As the st**
Florida,**
in compa
secure th

By the time the aluminum shutters covered all the windows, the sky had turned a leaden gray and the breeze had stiffened. Suddenly rain spattered, and we dashed to the front porch.

Bill gazed at the sky. "The first of the feeder bands has arrived. I'd better go."

He gathered me in his arms and kissed me until I couldn't breathe, then released me and sprinted down the walk. At the front gate he turned, rain streaming down his face, and shouted, "I love you, Margaret."

"I love you," I said, already missing his arms around me.

I realized then how foolish my earlier jealousy had been. At that moment I didn't worry that Bill might fall in love with his ex-wife. I simply prayed that he and all of us survived the coming storm and that I would see him again.

Charlotte Douglas

The major passions of Charlotte Douglas's life are her husband—her high school sweetheart to whom she's been married for over three decades—and writing compelling stories. A national bestselling author, she enjoys filling her books with love of home and family, special places and happy endings. With their two cairn terriers, she and her husband live most of the year on Florida's central west coast, but spend the warmer months at their North Carolina mountaintop retreat.

No matter what time of year, readers can reach her at charlottedouglas1@juno.com, where she's always delighted to hear from them.

Charlotte Douglas
STORM SEASON

STORM SEASON

copyright © 2007 by Charlotte H. Douglas

isbn-13:978-0-373-88137-6

isbn-10:   0-373-88137-1

TheNextNovel.com

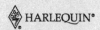 HARLEQUIN®

PRINTED IN U.S.A.

From the Author

Dear Reader,

For any Floridian who lived in the state during 2004–2005, two simple words now conjure dread and anxiety: hurricane season. Hundreds of thousands rode out storms in homes or shelters with windows shuttered, power down, all held hostage to the whim of nature. Some were luckier than others, but the trauma still lingers, and even the intrepid Maggie Skerritt isn't immune. Now storm warnings are flying in Pelican Bay, but weather isn't the only threat to Maggie.

After twenty-three years, Bill Malcolm's ex-wife reappears, wreaking havoc on Maggie and Bill's relationship. A homeless stranger with amnesia is a potential threat to the elderly Lassiter sisters, and Pelican Bay Investigations has a high-profile stalking case to solve. Add to these problems the unwanted amorous advances of sheriff detective Garrett Keating and a category-five hurricane and, as usual, Maggie has her hands full.

So batten down the hatches and join Maggie on her latest adventure.

Happy reading!

Charlotte Douglas

MAGGIE SKERRITT MYSTERIES
BY CHARLOTTE DOUGLAS
STORM SEASON
WEDDING BELL BLUES
SPRING BREAK
HOLIDAYS ARE MURDER
PELICAN BAY

Violet Lassiter passed me the heavy blue-willow plate with a remarkably steady hand for a one-hundred-year-old. "Have a cookie, Miss Skerritt."

She didn't have to twist my arm. Fresh from the oven, the cookies smelled heavenly.

"They're better with nuts," she added in apology, "but Bessie can't have 'em, so the rest of us have to suffer."

"You eat too many sweets, anyway," her eighty-four-year-old sibling, Bessie, countered.

"What do you think—" Violet accused her with a roll of her eyes "—that I'm going to shorten my life?"

Taking a cookie, I sat on the screened back porch of the modest cement-block home with the two elderly women, who were apparently unfazed by the ninety-degree heat and suffocating humidity of the September morning. Violet, tall and gangly with thick white braids wrapped around her head like a crown, wore a heavy sweater over her cotton housedress.

Bessie, short and lean, was also dressed in a cotton shift and a cardigan, plus bright-pink sneakers and heavy flesh-toned nylons rolled just below her knees.

I'd first encountered the Lassiter sisters last June when Bill Malcolm, my fiancé and partner in Pelican Bay Investigations, had done background checks on volunteers for the local historical society. To his dismay, he'd discovered that Bessie had an arrest record for shoplifting. Further digging revealed she'd been stealing food for Violet after their Social Security money had run out before the end of the month. The judge had given Bessie probation, but his lenient ruling hadn't solved the elderly women's subsistence problem.

Bill and I had arranged for meals-on-wheels for the pair and had put together a gift basket to tide them over until deliveries began. To save the Lassiters' pride, we'd fabricated a story that Bessie had won the basket in a grand opening raffle we'd held at our business. We'd presented them the basket of staples and goodies, along with our business card and instructions to call on us if they needed a private investigator, a request we never expected to receive.

Their call came yesterday.

I'd solved many cases during my twenty-three years as a cop and more recently for Pelican Bay Investigations, but I couldn't guess what dilemma had prompted these elderly sisters to contact me. And I couldn't get them to stop sniping at one another long enough to find out.

"Get Miss Skerritt more ice," Violet ordered her sister in a drill-sergeant tone. "Her tea's getting warm."

"Just because you're older doesn't mean you can boss me around," Bessie shot back.

"My tea is fine, really," I said. "Now what—"

"You need to be bossed," Violet said, ignoring me, "because you act like a child. I hope I live long enough to see you grow up."

"Ladies." I spoke loudly and firmly. The situation was spiraling out of control, sweat was soaking through the back of my blouse and all I could think of was how great air-conditioning would feel about now. "Why exactly did you want to see me?"

"We have a man," Bessie announced with a gleeful expression.

I nodded but didn't comment, not sure where this was going.

"A tenant," Violet corrected.

"But he's not a paying tenant," Bessie added. "More like a guest."

I gazed into the tiny house through the open back door but couldn't spot anyone inside, and I was beginning to wonder if this mysterious tenant wasn't senility's equivalent of an imaginary friend.

"Where is he?" I asked.

"Over there." Bessie pointed to a toolshed at the rear of the yard that backed up to the Pinellas Trail, a linear park built on an old railroad bed that ran the length of the county.

I narrowed my eyes, but the shed door was shut, and I caught no flicker of movement inside. With the windows closed and the Florida sun beating on the roof, the interior temperature had to be over a hundred degrees. If their "guest" was in there, he was well done by now.

"Oh…kay," I said, not wanting to call her crazy to her face.

"He's not there now, Bessie." Violet's condescending older sister voice reminded me of my own sibling, Caroline. "He's gone out."

"You have a man living in your garden shed?" I felt like Alice who'd tumbled down the rabbit hole.

Bessie nodded.

"What's his name?" The investigator in me couldn't help asking, while the saner part of my nature chided me for encouraging their delusions.

"He doesn't have a name," Violet said, "so we call him J.D."

Curiouser and curiouser. The ladies had obviously lost it.

"J.D. for John Doe," Bessie said. "He's a lovely man."

"Who doesn't have a name." An incipient ache flared behind my eyes.

"Well, he had a name at one time—" Violet began.

"—but he can't remember it," Bessie finished. "Can't remember anything. Who he is, where he came from, not even his age, although I'd put him in his early sixties, if I had to guess." She chomped the last bite of her third cookie, sans nuts.

"He has the nicest manners," Violet said, "or we wouldn't tolerate him. Why, for the longest time, we didn't even know he was there."

"We wouldn't have known at all," Bessie agreed, "if it hadn't been for the Turk's Cap bush."

Violet nodded.

I was beginning to wonder if I were the one losing it. Nothing either of them said made any sense.

"That bush grew so high during the summer rains," Bessie explained, "that it blocked the view from my bedroom window. So I went to the shed for the clippers."

"We don't use the shed much any longer," Violet said, "since that nice young neighbor—"

"Mr. Moore," Bessie said.

"Don't interrupt," her sister snapped.

"But you'd forgotten his name."

"I didn't forget. I hadn't gotten to it yet."

"So you don't use the shed…" I prompted Violet in hopes of ending the bickering.

Bessie answered. "Mr. Moore mows our grass when he does his yard. He's very thoughtful."

"Thoughtful, my eye," Violet said. "He got sick of looking at the jungle over here."

While Bessie searched for a suitable comeback, I plunged into the void. "What did you find in the shed, Bessie?"

"Come and see for yourself."

I set aside my glass of tea, pushed to my feet from the ancient metal glider and followed Bessie out the screen door. Violet, amazingly agile for a centenarian, dogged our steps as if afraid she'd miss something.

We followed a path of popcorn stone, set in thick St. Augustine grass, to the shed, constructed of the same concrete block as the house and apparently built at the same time, around 1940. The wooden door showed signs of rot, and several asphalt shingles were missing from the roof. A square of cardboard replaced a missing pane in one of two sash windows visible on the side of the shed that faced the house.

Bessie knocked on the door. "J.D., you home?"

When no one answered, she tugged open the warped door, reached inside and flipped a switch. Light from the bare bulb, which extended from a cord in the center of the ceiling, illuminated the opposite of what I'd expected.

Instead of a jumble of old tools, broken pots and other junk covered in dust and spiderwebs, the space was immaculate. The concrete floor had been recently swept, every surface dusted, the windowpanes sparkled in the sun and tools and garden implements hung in an orderly array on makeshift wall pegs. On an ancient wooden workbench in front of the east window sat rows of healthy green herbs in small pots. Next to the herbs were a single-burner electric hot plate, a battered but clean saucepan and a few cans of beans and franks. Beneath the bench stood a jug of drinking water and an old but sturdy Igloo cooler.

On the opposite side of the shed, under the west windows, a rough bed frame had been constructed from scraps of plywood and old lumber. Several ragged and faded blankets, neatly folded, lay beside a stained pillow. On a peg above the bed hung a heavy army jacket.

Either the Lassiter sisters had staged an elaborate set for their delusion, or the mysterious J.D. wasn't a figment of their imagination but real flesh and blood.

My concern for the frail and elderly ladies skyrocketed. "Have you called the sheriff's office?"

"Oh, no," Bessie said in a horrified tone.

"We wanted to," Violet said, "but police make J.D. nervous, poor man."

"So you want me to evict him?" I thought I'd finally gotten a handle on why the sisters had summoned me.

"Evict him?" Bessie's eyes widened with alarm. "Of course not. That would be inhospitable."

"We want you to find out who he is," Violet explained in the same exasperated voice she used on her sister. "He's such a dear man, we're sure he has a family somewhere who love him and miss him. In the meantime, we're happy to have him stay with us."

"We even offered to share our meals," Bessie added, "but he didn't want to impose."

"How does he support himself?" I asked.

"He doesn't beg, if that's what you're thinking," Violet said sharply.

The old lady was quick. That J.D. was a panhandler, at best, was exactly what I'd been thinking.

"He's too proud," Bessie said. "He'd never take charity. He insists on doing odd jobs around our house to pay his rent. He stopped our faucet from dripping, planed a closet door that always stuck and mended a window screen. He also trims the shrubbery and weeds the flower beds. And as soon as we can afford a new pane, he's going to repair the shed window."

"He has an old bicycle," Violet added. "He rides around town and collects aluminum cans. Then he takes them to the recycling center and sells them."

"I'm sure J.D. is very…nice." I was trying to be tactful. "But are you sure he's not dangerous?"

Violet drew herself to her full height, very imposing since it included six inches of braided coronet.

"Young lady, I didn't get to be a hundred years old without learning a few things. I am an excellent judge of character. J.D. may have forgotten who he is, but he hasn't forgotten what he is."

"And what's that?" I asked.

"A kind and gentle man who's temporarily lost his way," Violet said. "We asked you here to help him find it."

"Will you?" Bessie asked. "As much as we like having J.D., we do want him to find his family."

Faced with the Lassiters' sincere concern, I didn't have the heart to tell them that J.D. was most likely one of a vast army of homeless, many of whom, due to mental illness, had chosen life on the streets rather than deal with the strains and stresses of a normal life. I only hoped he wasn't also the type who suffered bouts of violence because he wasn't on medication.

"I'll have to meet J.D. and talk with him," I said. "Then I'll see what I can do. Can you call me when he's here?"

Bessie looked embarrassed.

Violet squared her shoulders and raised her chin. "We had the phone taken out. Never used it, except to answer calls from telemarketers."

I knew better. The Lassiters' fixed income hadn't stretched to include the monthly phone bill.

"Maybe your neighbor, Mr. Moore, will call me?" I suggested.

"That's a good idea," Bessie said. "He's already volunteered to call 9-1-1 if we ever need help. I'm sure he won't mind calling you."

I said goodbye, hurried to my ancient Volvo and cranked up the air-conditioning. I hoped J.D. returned soon, so I could meet him and decide whether to call the police, despite the sisters' objections, for their own safety.

As I drove away, I knew I wouldn't bill them for my time. As Bill always said, pro bono work was good for the soul.

Especially if it kept two lively old ladies out of harm's way.

CHAPTER 2

Darcy Wilkins, our receptionist and secretary, greeted me with a distracted wave when I returned to the office. She was eating lunch at her desk and watching the noon news on the small television in the waiting area. Roger, my three-year-old pug, showed more enthusiasm at my arrival and followed me toward my office.

"Look," Darcy said around a mouthful of yogurt, pointing to the TV with her spoon, "there's Adler."

Dave Adler had been my partner during my final months with the Pelican Bay Police Department. When the city had disbanded the PD and the sheriff's office had taken over, Adler had gone to work as a detective with the Clearwater Department.

I stopped midstride, pivoted and almost tripped over Roger in my haste to view the screen. Young enough to be my son, but already a stellar detective, Adler always evoked a certain maternal pride. Gazing at the screen where the Clearwater PD spokesperson was being interviewed, I could see Adler and his current partner, Ralph Porter, in the background, carrying evidence bags to their car, just as the news segment ended.

"Did you hear what was going on?" I asked Darcy.

"Murder on Sand Key. Some woman was shot when she got out of her car inside the gated lot at her condo."

My skin prickled at her words. But this homicide was Adler's problem, not mine, so the hives that usually erupted at the mention of murder remained dormant.

"It's too soon for the police to announce the victim's identity," I said. "Not until next of kin are notified."

Darcy scraped the bottom of her yogurt cup with her plastic spoon, gave the drooling Roger a lick and tossed the spoon and container into the trash. "No motive yet, either."

"Anyone see the shooter?"

"Not according to the newscast."

At one time, the killing would have led the news in Tampa Bay. But with growth in population had come a corresponding increase in crime. Murders were commonplace, and the report of this homicide had been delayed until right before the weather.

I glanced toward Bill's office and spotted his empty desk through the open door. I hadn't talked with him since the previous evening. "Any word from Bill?"

Darcy nodded. "He called right after you left for the Lassiters. Said he wouldn't be in this morning and asked that you meet him at the boat at three this afternoon."

When we'd parted last night, Bill had said he'd see me at the office this morning, so apparently something had come up. "Did he say where he was?"

Darcy shook her head.

"What he was doing?"

She shrugged. "He seemed distracted, in a hurry. That's all I know. I'm just the hired help. Nobody tells me anything."

I suppressed a smile. We usually didn't have to tell Darcy what was going on. She had the uncanny ability to hear whatever happened in the office, even behind closed doors.

"Any other calls?" I asked.

"No. It's been like the quiet before the storm."

"Bite your tongue. That's a word I don't want to hear until December." The first day of that month would mark the end of hurricane season.

I took a seat on the chair nearest Darcy's desk, faced the television and waited for the weather forecast. Early September is the peak of hurricane season, and for residents of Florida, that meant all eyes were on the tropics, and chief meteorologists Paul Dellegatto of FOX 13 and Steve Jerve of Channel 8 had become our best friends and constant companions.

So far this season, South Florida and the panhandle had been hit hard. Tampa Bay residents were holding their collective breath, wondering if this would be the year of the Big One, when a storm the equivalent of Ivan or Katrina would wreak havoc on an area that had been spared destruction since 1921.

Bill and I always remained alert to the changing weather. Living aboard his cabin cruiser at the Pelican Bay Marina, Bill needed plenty of lead time to secure his boat before evacuating. And my waterfront condo was in a mandatory evacuation zone. Before the multiple hits Florida took in 2004, I'd been more casual about leaving when a storm was forecast. But after viewing pictures of houses near the water that Ivan and Katrina had obliterated, except for the concrete slab foundations, I'd developed a healthier respect for the storms' potential for damage. Every June when hurricane season began, I packed a large plastic bin with important papers, canned goods, bottled water, battery-powered lanterns, a first aid kit and kibble for Roger and stored it in the hall closet, ready to set in the car and evacuate at a moment's notice.

On the little TV, the commercial ended and the weather forecast began.

"Damn," I said.

The icon for a tropical storm had popped up on the weather map south of Jamaica in the Caribbean. The cone of probability for Tropical Storm Harriet stretched five days out and indicated the storm would strengthen in intensity and, pushed by upper air currents, a shifting jet stream and meandering Bermuda High, curve back toward Florida. For now, the state's west coast, from the Dry Tortugas all the way to Cedar Key, was on alert.

Darcy sighed. "Now we'll be glued to the television for days."

"Yeah, praying it misses us and feeling guilty for wishing it on some other part of the country." I stood up and headed for my office. "Come on, Roger, we have work to do."

By work, I meant reading the *Times* and the *Tribune* and finishing the crossword puzzles, because, except for eventually identifying the Lassiter sisters' tenant, I had no active cases at the moment. The hiatus didn't disturb me. I had my police pension and a small trust fund from my father. Bill also had his police pension and a small fortune in real estate in the orange groves his father had left him. Pelican Bay Investigations was more a venture to keep us both busy and sane rather than a needed source of income.

A LITTLE BEFORE THREE, I set aside the completed puzzles, put a leash on Roger, told Darcy I wouldn't be in again until the next morning and drove a few blocks to the marina. Anvil-shaped clouds towered in the eastern sky and portended evening thunderstorms. In spite of the threatening weather, many of the slips at the marina were empty due to sailors enjoying pleasure cruises and charter boat captains fulfilling the fishing fantasies of tourists in the deep waters of the Gulf.

Bill's thirty-eight-foot cabin cruiser, *Ten-Ninety-Eight*, police code for "mission accomplished," was docked at the end of one of several piers. It appeared closed and deserted, but as Roger and I approached, I could hear the hum of air-conditioning. I'd already spotted Bill's SUV in the parking lot, so I knew he was aboard. I stepped from the dock to the rear deck and tapped on the sliders that opened onto the lounge, Bill's tiny but efficient living area.

When he opened the glass door, my heart did a little flip-flop at the sight of him, making me feel like a teenager again instead of a forty-nine-year-old. Even at sixty, Bill was a man who turned women's heads. Tall, tan and in terrific shape, with thick white hair and blue eyes, he grew more handsome with age. But today those baby blues had no twinkle when they greeted me, and his usual grin had gone AWOL.

"You okay?" I asked.

He pulled me inside, closed the door behind Roger and grabbed me in a brief but fierce hug.

"We have to talk." His tone was as serious as his expression.

Fear threatened to close my throat. For years, Bill had been pressuring me to marry him. Set in my single ways and commitment-shy, I'd dragged my feet until recently. Last Christmas, we'd set our wedding date for Valentine's Day, still five months away, to give me time to get used to the idea of marriage, but after we'd solved our last case, I'd recognized my delaying tactics as senseless. I wanted to spend the rest of my life with Bill, and we weren't getting any younger, so what was I waiting for? We'd agreed then that we'd marry as soon as we finished furnishing the house we'd bought together a few months earlier.

Except for a few odds and ends, the house was now move-in ready. Judging by his expression, I worried now that Bill was the one getting cold feet.

I sank onto the love seat on one side of the lounge, and Bill took one of the folding director's chairs across the room from me. Not a good sign.

"I'm listening," I said.

Roger curled onto the sofa next to me and placed his head on my lap, as if sensing I needed comfort.

Bill's face looked pained. "I don't know how to say this."

In spite of his tan, his skin had a strange pallor. I prayed he wasn't ill. I snapped my mind shut against a dozen dire possibilities.

"Just tell me."

He took a deep breath and exhaled, like a diver getting ready to take a header off the tower. "It's Trish."

The years fell away, and I was once again a rookie, fresh out of the academy, with Bill Malcolm as my first partner with the Tampa Police Department. He had a wife the other male officers envied, a gorgeous woman with magnificent red hair, exotic green eyes, a curvaceous figure and a sense of humor that kept everyone around her smiling. Bill and Trish also had a six-year-old daughter, Melanie. The perfect family.

Until the strain of having a husband who put his life on the line every day finally broke Trish's nerves and their marriage. The end came right after I'd saved

Bill from being hacked to death by a machete-wielding wife abuser. I'd had to put three rounds in the guy's chest to stop him, the only time in my career I'd ever fired my weapon. Bill was safe, but the what-might-have-been had sent Trish over the edge. She filed for divorce, moved to Seattle and took their daughter Melanie with her.

And she'd broken Bill's heart. He had still loved her and eventually had come to realize that she'd loved him, too, and the only way she could end the marriage that was destroying her emotionally had been to put a continent between them.

At first, Melanie had returned to Tampa for summer visits with her dad, but as she reached adolescence, she had wanted to remain in Seattle with her friends—and her stepfather. Trish's new husband, an accountant, had a nice safe job where no one would try to kill him, unless he was caught cooking the books by a client with a temper and the means for murder—highly unlikely for the straight-arrow Harvey in his safe suburban practice.

So over the twenty-three years since the divorce, Bill had lost touch with both Trish and Melanie and, to my amazement and delight, had fallen in love with me. Even when Melanie had married and had had children, she hadn't encouraged her father to participate in their lives, a crying shame since Bill would have been a first-class grandfather.

"What about Trish?" I asked.

My first thought had been that she'd died. She was Bill's contemporary, after all, and not everyone lived to the ripe old age of the Lassiter sisters.

He spread his hands in a gesture of either appeal or frustration. I couldn't tell. "She's back."

"Back in Tampa?"

He shook his head, looking more uncomfortable than I'd ever seen him.

Roger, sensing the tension crackling in the tiny cabin, sat up and looked from me to Bill and back and whined softly.

A devastating second thought hit me. "Trish is back with you?"

"God, no," Bill said immediately and with such emphasis, I exhaled in relief. "But it's complicated."

"Apparently," I said with too much sarcasm, "or I'd have some clue what the hell is going on. You said Trish is back. Exactly where is she?"

The pained expression returned to Bill's face, but he raised his chin and looked me in the eye. "She's living in our house."

CHAPTER 3

"What?" I shook my head, thinking I'd heard wrong.

"I left her there until I could talk with you."

"You left your ex-wife in our house?" I couldn't believe it. The entire exchange sounded like the script for a bad soap opera. "Why?"

"Harvey dumped her for a younger model."

"So she's come running back to you?" Insecurity gripped me. Bill had loved Trish, she was the mother of his only child, and now she wasn't just a distant memory three thousand miles away. She was right here in Pelican Bay.

In *our* house.

"She called late last night, hysterical," he explained. "Not only did Harvey leave her for a younger woman, but he'd planned every detail of his escape before Trish had a hint that anything was wrong. The creep cleaned out their joint accounts and canceled her credit cards. The deed to their house was already in Harvey's name only, and he demanded that she move out. What could I do? Trish had nowhere to go."

"She has a daughter."

Bill pushed his fingers through his hair and frowned. "Trish called Melanie, but Melanie sided with Harvey. Said if Trish had been a better wife, Harvey wouldn't have left her. Trish asked Melanie if she could stay with her until she can get back on her feet, but Melanie told her that in her present emotional state, Trish would upset the children."

Years ago, Bill and I had often discussed how Trish had spoiled Melanie, as if trying to make up to her daughter for the divorce. Now Melanie's resulting self-centeredness was coming back to bite her mother.

"Trish was desperate, or she wouldn't have called me," Bill said. "And she is the mother of my only child. What else could I do?" he repeated.

He could have hung up on her, I thought, like I would have. But Bill was a better person than I'd ever be, another of the reasons I loved him so much.

"I wired her money for a plane ticket," he continued, "picked her up at the Tampa Airport at noon and left her at the house until I could talk to you."

"You could have taken her to a motel."

"I tried, but Labor Day weekend's coming up. Every decent motel or hotel in the area is booked solid."

"How long do you intend for her to stay at our place?" I tried but couldn't keep the hostility from my voice.

Bill rose from his chair, crossed the cabin, sat next to me, and took both my hands in his. "I love you, Margaret. Whatever there was between Trish and me is over and done. Dead. I'm not the same man I was all those years ago."

But he'd loved Trish before, a nagging little voice in my head insisted. And if he's around her long enough, he might love her again.

"If you don't want her in our house," he said, "say the word. I'll find someplace else, even if I have to rent Abe Mackley's guest room."

Abe, now retired, had been a detective with us in Tampa. I doubted his wife wanted Trish around any more than I did.

"What's your plan?" I knew Bill wouldn't have brought Trish all the way across the country without some thought of what to do with her once she arrived.

"First, find her another place to stay. Our house is only temporary until she can locate an apartment. I'll loan her some funds until she can get a job and pay me back."

"What kind of job?" Breaking into the workforce at sixty was no easy feat.

"Trish was a secretary in a law firm before we married," Bill said.

"Typewriters ruled in those days." I shook my head. "She'll need training, unless she's already learned computer skills and the necessary programs."

"Then she can sign up for courses at the Clearwater campus of St. Petersburg College."

Knowing Bill, he'd pay for that, too. Here I was, figuratively rubbing my hands with glee over what-goes-around-comes-around, while he, the person Trish had hurt the most, was bending over backward to bail her out of deep doo-doo. I should have been ashamed.

But I wasn't.

"It's up to you, Margaret," he said.

"Why me? She's your ex-wife."

"Because you're the most important person in my life, and I won't do anything that would hurt you or make you uncomfortable."

Great. All I had to do was say the word. Bill would leave Trish to fend for herself, and I'd spend the rest of my days feeling like the world's most selfish bitch.

I tried to shove emotion aside and let reason reign. What harm would it do to let Trish stay in our house a few days until she could find her own place? Bill and I hadn't planned to move in for a few more weeks.

And just because Trish had been heartless all those years ago didn't mean I had to follow her example. If Bill could forgive her and show compassion, so could I.

"You're right," I said, feeling magnanimous. "We'd be cruel not to help her."

He enveloped me in his arms, and his lips brushed my ear. "I knew you'd understand. You're a good woman, and I'm a damned lucky man to have you. It'll all work out, you'll see."

I wished I shared his optimism. I saw potential disaster no matter what decision I made, and I wouldn't rest easy until the glamorous Trish was once again out of our lives and, preferably, at least three thousand miles away again.

Bill released me. "We'll take Trish to dinner tonight to try to cheer her up."

I stifled a groan. Talk about a rock and a hard place. I didn't want to socialize with Bill's ex, but I didn't want him alone with her, either. I was mulling over which was the lesser of two evils when Bill's cell phone rang.

He answered and handed it to me. "It's Darcy."

"I've got a hysterical woman on the other line," Darcy said.

My first thought was that Trish had called the office.

"She says somebody's trying to kill her," Darcy added.

"Tell her to call 9-1-1."

"I already did. She claims she's talked to the police and there's nothing they can do. She wants to talk to you."

"Make her an appointment for first thing in the morning."

"Tried that. She wants to see you now. Says she needs a bodyguard." Darcy paused. "She's either a total weirdo or really scared out of her mind, Maggie. I can't tell which over the phone."

"Give me her address," I said with a sigh. One dilemma, at least, was solved. If I was interviewing Darcy's caller, I wouldn't have to go to dinner with Bill and Trish.

"Her name's Kimberly Ross," Darcy said, "and she lives in the penthouse at Sun and Sea condos on Sand Key."

"Tell Ms. Ross I'm on my way." I pushed End and gave Bill his phone and a summary of Darcy's message. "I'll have to pass on dinner. Can you take care of Roger? I don't know how long this will take."

"Of course." He grasped my chin and tipped my face to look into my eyes. "You sure you're okay with this Trish thing?"

"No," I answered honestly, "and I need time to

think about it. But the woman has to eat, so I have no objection to your taking her to dinner."

Okay, so that second part wasn't so honest, but with Trish back in the picture, the last thing I wanted was to come across as an insensitive jerk or rabidly jealous. I'd wait, assess the situation and then, if I thought Trish posed the slightest threat to our relationship, I'd scratch her gorgeous green eyes out.

"You're the best, Margaret." Bill kissed me to back up his words.

Leaving Roger with Bill and heading for my car, I could only hope, with Trish back in town, that I maintained that ranking.

GOING-HOME TRAFFIC was heavy on Edgewater Drive all the way through downtown Clearwater and across the arching bridge that led to the causeway and the beach. I crossed the causeway, navigated the roundabout and headed south on Gulf Boulevard. Beach real estate was in a state of flux. Where mom-and-pop motels and restaurants had once stood, land had been cleared for multistory luxury condos. In the coming years, families that now swarmed the area for a last fling before going back to school would find no affordable places to vacation. Only the rich and richer would be able to afford living on the beach. That famous white sugar sand might as well be gold dust.

I crossed the Clearwater Pass Bridge onto Sand Key and watched for the sign for Sun and Sea among the towers of condos on the Gulf side. I found the complex south of the Sheraton and turned into the drive. When I pulled up to the entrance, yellow crime scene tape flapped in the onshore breeze just inside the gate.

Although I'd never been here, the parking lot seemed vaguely familiar. Then recognition clicked.

No wonder the woman who'd called the office was scared. Sun and Sea had been the location of the shooting Darcy and I had seen reported on the noon news. I waited while the security guard buzzed Ms. Ross for permission to admit me, drove through after he opened the gate and searched for a parking place.

A Clearwater police cruiser was parked in front of the visitor spaces and a uniformed officer stood outside his car, leaning against the hood. I recognized Rudy Beaton, a former Pelican Bay cop, and rolled down my window.

"How about moving that heap of junk so a lady can park?" I called to him.

"Maggie? Is that you?" Beaton pushed away from his vehicle and approached mine.

"I'm here to call on a client," I said. "Good to see you. How's the job treating you?"

He grinned. "You know how it is. I'm counting the days till retirement."

I jerked my thumb toward the yellow tape. "Did you respond to the shooting?"

Beaton shook his head. "That was before my shift. I'm here to keep an eye on the scene until CSU has finished up."

I glanced around. "Looks like they've already left."

He pointed to a hotel south of the condo. "They're processing a room over there. Fifth floor."

"That's where the sniper fired from?"

"Doc Cline and Adler are working that theory," Beaton said.

Doc Cline was the medical examiner. She and Adler must have calculated the trajectory of the bullet that killed the woman earlier today.

"Did the vic live here?" I asked.

Beaton shook his head. "She was from out of town, here to visit relatives for the weekend."

I looked from the hotel window to the parking lot where the woman had died. "Guess that put a crimp in their holiday plans."

"You ever see any of the guys from Pelican Bay…" he asked with a hint of nostalgia "…other than Adler and Darcy?"

"Not lately. Seems as if they've scattered to the four

winds." Political maneuvering under the guise of saving money had shut down the Pelican Bay Police Department earlier in the year and had left everyone from uniformed officers and detectives to support personnel scrambling for new jobs.

"Me, either. Except for Adler." Beaton's face reflected the sadness I felt over the breakup, like a family that had suffered through a nasty divorce. "I'll move my cruiser," he said, "so you can park."

Rudy returned to his car, drove it away from the visitor parking and I pulled into a space.

Within minutes, I was exiting the condo's elevator onto the penthouse floor, twenty stories above the narrow strip of beach that edged the Gulf of Mexico.

At my knock, a woman with frizzy blond hair, wide gray eyes, stylish gold-framed glasses and tear-splotched cheeks, opened the door.

"Thank God you're here," she said. "I've been going out of my mind."

"You told my secretary someone's trying to kill you?" I glanced past her into the spacious living area and saw no other occupants. "Is everything okay here?"

As a former cop, I'd made my share of calls to sort out domestic disputes, and I didn't want to be surprised by a Mr. Kimberly Ross jumping out of the woodwork with blood in his eyes.

"No, everything isn't okay." Her voice shook with emotion. "The woman who was killed in the parking lot this morning wasn't the real target. That was supposed to be me."

CHAPTER 4

Kimberly Ross appeared to be in her early forties, but with her face puffy from crying, I couldn't accurately judge. She wore designer jeans that revealed her tendency toward pudginess and a gauzy tunic top. Her feet were bare. If she'd applied makeup earlier, her tears had obliterated every trace. Her square jaw and wide brow gave her a somewhat masculine appearance and, under different circumstances, her face could have been pleasant, but fear contorted her features and rolled off her in palpable waves.

"I came as fast as I could," I assured her in my most soothing tone, hoping to help the woman pull herself together before she lost it completely, because she was teetering on the edge of hysteria. "Why don't you fill me in on the details?"

"Come in." Kimberly stepped aside in the marble foyer for me to enter.

I followed her into the expansive living room with a soaring vaulted ceiling and was blown away by the view. Her condo filled the twentieth story, and floor-to-ceiling glass on both ends of the living area presented endless views of the Gulf on the west and a panorama of Clearwater Harbor on the east. The walls and plush carpet were pale lavender, the same tone as the modern upholstered furniture. Throw pillows in pastel pinks, yellows and blues and an oversize oil painting in matching hues above the pink marble fireplace were the only visual relief from the unrelenting lavender. I felt as if I had stepped into a gigantic Easter basket. The only things missing were fake grass and chocolate bunnies.

Kimberly waved me to a chair and curled into the corner of the sofa nearest me. My presence must have eased some of her fears, because she'd calmed somewhat, even though her hands still trembled. "Thank you for coming so quickly."

I nodded. "You want to tell me what this is about?"

"Detective Adler recommended you."

"You spoke with him?"

"I didn't know about the murder in the parking lot until he knocked at my door. He said they were questioning everyone in the building, but I hadn't seen or heard anything."

"Did you know the victim?"

The muscles of her face flinched, and her lower lip

quivered, threatening fresh tears. She nodded. "Sister Mary Theresa, such a sweet woman."

"Somebody shot a nun?"

Kimberly nodded again and hooked strands of kinky hair behind her ears. "Her parents, Dennis and Eileen Moynihan, live on the second floor. Their daughter was here from Boston for her annual visit. Now they'll be taking her back to Massachusetts to bury her."

If Doc Cline and Adler's theory was correct, the killer had waited in a hotel room next door for his victim. The shooting appeared planned, not random.

"Who'd want to kill a nun?" I asked.

"Nobody. They wanted to kill me, but poor Mary Theresa died instead."

Hoping to nip her waterworks in the bud, I asked, "Why are you so certain you were the target?"

Kimberly took a deep, shuddering breath. "Mary Theresa and I look enough alike to be twins. Dennis and Eileen were struck by the resemblance the first time I met them when I moved in three years ago. In fact, they call me their other daughter and fuss over me as if we really are related. And, like you said, who'd want to kill a nun?"

"The better question, then, is who would want to kill you?"

She unfolded her legs from beneath her and stood. "Come with me."

I followed her through the lavender and pastel haze to a set of frosted-glass double doors. She threw them open and motioned me inside the large but windowless room, illuminated by a huge skylight. A customized maple workstation curved around one corner and was topped by a computer, fax machine, printer, scanner and multiline telephone. Bulletin boards above the work area bristled with papers and notes of every size and color, held in place by pushpins. A set of ceiling-high shelves, crammed with books, filled the opposite wall, and tall file cabinets flanked both sides of the workstation.

I was the detective, but I didn't have a clue. "Someone wants to kill you because you work at home?"

Kimberly brushed past me, picked up a newspaper clipping from the desktop and handed it to me. It was the latest copy of "Ask Wynona Wisdom," a syndicated advice column that ran in newspapers all over the country. More than simply advice to the lovelorn, the column fielded questions on every aspect of life, from decorating and pet problems to etiquette and family relationships. Wynona Wisdom was an expert on everything, and the reading public had devoured her opinions for more than fifteen years. I'd felt moved on several occasions to write to her concerning my overbearing mother but, so far, had resisted the temptation. A few words on a page couldn't do justice to the complexity of my maternal parent, a travel agent for guilt trips.

I glanced at the column again, and Wynona's picture, a thumb-sized cut, stared back at me.

"That's you," I said.

"I'm Wynona," she admitted. "And along with hundreds of letters every day asking for advice, I also receive death threats. I bet Sister Mary Theresa never had a death threat. Hell, she probably never had anyone raise a voice to her. So which one of us do you think is the likeliest candidate to be murdered?"

The woman had a point. "Did you explain all this to Detective Adler?"

Kimberly nodded. "And I told him I needed round-the-clock protection. That's when he suggested I call you. As soon as the media get hold of Mary Theresa's identity, the killer will know he missed his target and will come back after me."

She left her office, closed the doors, and I followed her into the living room. By now the sun was dipping lower in the west, casting blinding light straight through the penthouse. Kimberly pressed a remote control on the table beside the sofa, and sheer lavender draperies swished closed against the glare.

I returned to my chair. "You can't rule out completely that the nun was the target. Or that the killing was random. Remember the snipers in the Maryland area a few years back? Or, more recently, in Phoenix? They didn't know their victims. They just shot whoever was handy for the sheer terror it caused."

"I know." Kimberly plopped onto the sofa. "But while the police are sorting this out, I don't want to take a chance."

"Understood," I said. "Our firm can arrange to have someone with you 24-7."

With other clients, I would have mentioned how costly that level of protection would be, but judging from Kimberly's lucrative profession and lavish penthouse, I figured she could afford it.

"Starting now?" she asked.

"Starting now. Can I use your phone?"

She pointed toward her office. "It's in there."

FIFTEEN MINUTES LATER after completing my calls, I found Kimberly in the kitchen.

"You hungry?" she asked.

"Sure."

Mainly I was being sociable. Thinking about Bill

and Trish heading out to dinner together right about now had taken the edge off my appetite. I only hoped he wasn't planning on sitting with his ex-wife in our special booth at the Dock of the Bay. It was bad enough that the woman was living in our house.

I'd called Darcy and asked her to go by my condo and pack me a bag. She had a key for emergencies such as this and, happy to log in the overtime, would deliver the clothes and toiletries I'd requested to the penthouse later. I'd also instructed her to tell Bill where I was and that I'd be here overnight. I could have called Bill myself but hadn't wanted to interrupt his dinner plans with Trish. Call me crazy, but I'd rather not know where they were and what they were doing.

I climbed onto a high stool at the breakfast bar and watched Kimberly remove food from the refrigerator and pantry. She piled cold cuts onto thick slices of bread, smeared them with mayonnaise, heaped the plates high with chips and pickles and opened a bag of chocolate chip cookies and another of oatmeal-raisin.

She set one of the gargantuan sandwiches and potato chip mountains in front of me. "Iced tea or soda?"

"Diet Coke or water's fine."

She must have seen me eyeing the feast that would have fed four linebackers.

"When I'm anxious, I eat," she explained.

"I'd be the same way, but there's usually no food in my house. I hate to shop."

She sat across the bar from me and dug into her sandwich. If how much she consumed was a true sign of anxiety, Kimberly was almost ready for the psych ward. Between bites, she asked, "Do you carry a gun?"

I nodded.

"Where is it?"

"In the holster at the back of my waist. Don't worry. I can reach it in a hurry if I need it. But you have three levels of protection before anyone can get to me: the security officer at the gate, the private elevator that needs your personal code to activate it and the double deadlocks on your front doors. Unless some guy swoops onto your balcony from a helicopter, I won't be needing my weapon."

Her faced paled. She set her sandwich down and gazed toward the windows, covered with lavender fabric, as if she expected an assassin to crash through the glass sliders at any moment.

"Relax," I said. "Helicopter assaults happen only in the movies. Unless Bruce Willis or Steven Seagal is your hit man, you're perfectly safe."

I couldn't tell if my witty assurances made her feel more secure, since she returned to eating with renewed gusto.

I slid off the bar stool.

"Where are you going?" she asked in a panic. "You're not leaving?"

"I'm checking the locks."

I'd already stated how unlikely an attack was at twenty stories up, but she'd hired me for protection, so I went through the motions, if for no other reason than to make her feel better. After securing every glass slider and double-checking the dead bolts on the double front doors, I returned to the breakfast bar and my sandwich.

I didn't mention that, if her assailant had formerly served in special forces, twenty stories would be no deterrent, but how many SEALs, recon Marines or Army rangers had time to read "Ask Wynona Wisdom," much less work themselves into a killing lather over her advice?

My sweep of the room apparently reassured Kimberly, because she visibly relaxed. The only residual sign of anxiety was the rapidly disappearing cache of cookies.

She finished off an oatmeal-raisin in two bites. "I've never met a private eye before. Your job must be exciting."

"It's mostly paperwork. Background checks, tracking down lost relatives." After finally calming her down, I didn't want to ruin the result by sharing some of my more harrowing cases.

"Was this job, being an investigator, something you always wanted to do?"

At the rate she was paying me, talk wasn't cheap, but if conversation kept her mind off her worries, I'd humor her. "I started out as a librarian."

"Really? Why the major shift in careers?"

The passing years had eased the pain to a dull ache, so I could talk about Greg without feeling as if someone had ripped out my heart. "After I graduated from college and started working at the library, my fiancé, a doctor, was killed in the E.R. by a crack addict."

"How awful." My story momentarily distracted Kimberly from the cookies.

I nodded. "I was so angry about such a senseless waste, I had to do something, so I quit my library job and entered the police academy."

"You were a cop?"

"For over twenty-three years. Detective Adler was my last partner before I retired from the Pelican Bay Department. Then Bill Malcolm and I opened our agency earlier this year. What about you?"

"Me?"

"How did you become Wynona Wisdom?"

She made a face, as if the memories were unpleasant. "I got my PhD in psychology and opened my own counseling practice. But I couldn't stand the continual misery, day after day of listening to people pour out their problems. Guess you and I are alike in that sense. People don't come to counselors or cops unless they're in trouble."

She had that right. "But as Wynona Wisdom, you still deal with their misery every day, at least on paper."

She flashed a rueful smile. "I provide insight or give advice, but I don't have to watch people self-destruct by ignoring it."

I understood. Having clients unable to grasp, and therefore change, the circumstances that caused their problems was probably as frustrating for psychologists as recidivism was for cops, who often arrested people only to have them commit the same crimes again as soon as their sentences had been served.

"You must get a ton of mail," I said. "How do you keep up with it?"

"I have a staff of seven in Omaha. That's where I'm from, originally. They maintain the office there, sift through the letters, discard questions similar to ones I've answered before and send me the queries that are the most timely or interesting. They also help with research, if I need it."

"And the death threats?"

"They keep a file of those, just in case."

"You never read them?"

Kimberly shook her head and reached for another cookie. "I used to, but they were too upsetting. So upsetting, in fact, that I decided to relocate here, become more anonymous."

"No one's ever bothered you here?"

She shook her head. "Not until today. I guess you cops would say my cover's blown."

"That's only if the shooter was really after you. We haven't established that yet." I took a bite of sandwich, chewed and swallowed. "The death threats, the ones you used to read, what was the basis for them?"

She laughed without humor. "Most of the psychos didn't need a basis. One said my picture gave her the evil eye, staring out of her newspaper every morning. Another said he'd followed my advice about not letting his cat roam outdoors, and the feline had died of a broken heart and boredom. And there are always the wackos who say I should roast in hell for getting rich off of other people's misery."

"Did you save those letters?"

"My staff saves them."

"And the envelopes?"

She nodded.

I checked my watch. Six-thirty. It would be five-thirty in Omaha, and FedEx didn't close until after seven. "Can you call your office, have them box up all the threatening letters and overnight them?"

"Sure, my chief assistant will take care of it. Damn." She shook her head. "I keep forgetting Steve's on vacation, but Cindy can handle it. She's not as efficient as Steve, but this she can manage. But I don't know what good having the letters will do. Most of them are anonymous."

"You say someone wants to kill you. Part of my job is to find out who and, for now, those letters are the only clues we have." A thought struck me. "Unless you're involved in a family dispute. Or have relatives in your will who are overeager to inherit."

Kimberly shook her head. "My parents are dead, I have no siblings and my only living relative is a great-aunt with dementia who lives in a nursing home in Des Moines."

I waved my arm, encompassing the penthouse in my gesture. "You're obviously a wealthy woman. Who gets all this when you're gone?"

I could see the hackles rising on her neck. "That's a bit personal, isn't it?"

"Having me or another of my investigators sticking

to you like a second skin to keep you alive and well is about as personal as it gets," I said. "You can hire bodyguards to live in your pocket the rest of your life, or we can try to figure out—if you really were the killer's target—who had a reason to take a shot at you. Then we find him and free you to live normally."

Or as normal as life could be if you were Wynona Wisdom.

She groaned and buried her face in her hands. "I don't like to think about him, much less talk about him."

"Him, who?"

"My ex."

"Ex-husband?"

She lifted her head and grimaced. "We never got that far, thank God."

"I take it your parting wasn't amicable?"

"Amicable? It wasn't even civil."

"How uncivil was it?"

Kimberly's gray eyes widened. "He threatened to kill me."

CHAPTER 5

One of the ironies of interrogation that I'd discovered over the years was that people seldom tell you what you need to know up front. Often only after endless hours of careful probing does the blooming obvious finally surface.

"Tell me about your ex."

Kimberly made a face. "Like I said, I don't like to talk about him."

"A disgruntled partner from a former relationship should top our list of suspects."

"But Simon wasn't serious about killing me. He was just angry because I'd broken our engagement. And that was three years ago, right before I left Omaha. He's moved on by now."

"You're sure?" I wondered how much her broken relationship had factored into her move to Florida.

Kimberly shrugged and reached for another cookie. If Adler and Porter didn't collar Sister Mary Theresa's shooter soon, Kimberly was going to need a new set of clothes in a larger size.

"What's Simon's last name and where does he live?" I asked.

"Anderson. And the last I knew, he was still living in Omaha and working as an investment counselor."

"Let me guess. You met him when you were looking for someone to manage the bundles you were earning as Wynona Wisdom."

Kimberly dusted cookie crumbs from her hands. "You want some coffee?"

"Thanks, and the more caffeine, the better." At the slow and painful rate that I was extracting needed information, it was going to be a long night.

Kimberly abandoned the rapidly diminishing supply of cookies, scooped coffee grounds into a filtered basket and filled the reservoir with water. With brewed coffee trickling into the glass carafe, she puttered around the kitchen, clearing plates, putting mayonnaise and leftover cold cuts into the fridge and placing the half-empty bag of chips in the pantry. I didn't have to be Sherlock Holmes to know she was stalling. Obviously, Simon was a sore point.

When the coffee had brewed, Kimberly filled two large ceramic mugs, also lavender, and offered cream and sugar. I heaped three spoonfuls of the sweetener into my coffee, then followed her into the living room. I took the chair I'd used earlier, and she settled once again into the corner of the sofa. She cradled the huge mug in both hands and sipped slowly. Sensing she wouldn't talk until she was ready, I waited.

"I met Simon at Starbucks," she finally said, "around the corner from my office in Omaha. We used to run into each other every morning on our way to work."

Her expression turned dreamy with memory. "He was so good-looking, I never thought he'd be interested in me, but one morning I dropped my purse. The contents scattered everywhere, and Simon got down on his hands and knees to help retrieve them." She smiled, but not at me. Her expression was distant, as if she was lost in the past, reliving the experience.

"I thanked him and apologized for being such a klutz. He said he was glad it had happened, that he'd been waiting for a chance to meet me. He'd recognized me from my picture in the paper." She looked at me and blushed. "He said he could tell from my columns that I was a fascinating woman."

"So he had no ulterior motive?" I said.

"What do you mean?"

"He never asked to handle your investments?"

Her flush deepened. "Well, yes, but only after we'd gone out together a few times."

Poor Wynona Wisdom, I thought. All that sage advice for others, and she'd walked straight into the arms of a disaster she hadn't seen coming. "And I bet you were one of his biggest accounts."

She nodded. "He was so grateful. If it hadn't been for me, he wouldn't have been promoted so quickly."

"And when you realized he was after you for your money, you dropped him?"

Her face reflected sadness, embarrassment and remorse. "I didn't recognize the financial implications of his interest in me until after the breakup. Funny, isn't it, how much easier it is to recognize other people's problems than your own?"

I dipped my head in agreement and thought about Bill and Trish. Did I really have a problem or, in a few days, as soon as Bill found his ex-wife a place to live, would she be out of our lives again with Bill and me back to making wedding plans?

"If you didn't think Simon was gold-digging," I said, "why did you break off your engagement?"

Kimberly stared into her coffee mug as if looking for answers. "At first, I was flattered by how attentive he was. You'd think that I, who'd advised so many women to run for their lives from controlling, abusive men, would have recognized the danger signals, but I was as blinded by love and denial as the next woman.

It wasn't until Simon blew up at me for not replacing the two young men on my staff with female employees that I became aware of what he really was."

"That must have been a scary realization."

"A reality check. How he could be jealous of Steve and Gerry, I couldn't figure. Steve is a terrific employee. Several years ago, when I was hospitalized with an emergency appendectomy and a post-op infection, Steve stepped in and wrote my column for six weeks. A nice guy, but he's years younger than me and not particularly attractive. And Gerry's obviously and flamboyantly gay. The fact that Simon was jealous of those two was a real wake-up call."

This time her smile was sly. "I made my moves before he knew what hit him. Within twenty-four hours, I'd switched my investments to another firm, changed all the locks on my office and apartment doors, arranged for new, unlisted phone numbers and booked a flight to Tampa to look for a place to live."

"And avoided the Starbucks around the corner?"

"Absolutely. I returned Simon's ring by messenger. The only contact I had with him after that was outside my apartment when I was getting into the cab for the drive to the airport. Simon was waiting. He grabbed me, called me every name in the book and threatened to kill me if I didn't marry him."

"Did you call the police?"

Kimberly shook her head and smiled. "Didn't have to. The cab driver was the size of a sumo wrestler. He told Simon if he didn't back off his fare, he'd mop the street with him. Simon was enraged, but he wasn't stupid. He knew he was no match for the cabbie."

"And you never heard from Simon again?"

"I just added his threatening letters to the pile with those from other wackos." She frowned. "What I'm telling you is confidential, you know?"

I crossed my heart. "Like attorney-client privilege. Our agency is discreet. But we should tell Detective Adler about Simon Anderson so he can check him out."

Kimberly thought for a moment. "Okay, but I don't think Simon shot Sister Mary Theresa."

"Because he knew she wasn't you?"

"Because if Simon is twisted enough to really want to hurt me, his type would want it up close and personal. Like any control freak, he feeds off fear. He'd want to see my terror, witness my suffering. Then he'd kill me. No, he wouldn't take a shot from a distance."

Sometimes knowing too much about what makes people tick could scare the daylights out of you. I attempted to lighten the conversation. "You called Simon a control freak. Is that a clinical diagnosis?"

She smiled. "It's God's honest truth."

"With your permission, I'll tell Adler."

"It's probably a waste of time. Simon's moved on to another victim by now."

Kimberly was already rattled, so I kept my theories about cold revenge to myself.

BEFORE EIGHT THE NEXT morning, I was headed back to my office. I'd called Abe Mackley from the penthouse the night before. Since Abe's retirement, he'd been happy to supplement his pension by working occasional assignments for our agency. Today he'd agreed to guard Kimberly at the penthouse while I did some digging into the nun's murder and Simon Anderson's background.

When I entered the office, Roger greeted me with a howl of delight. It was nice to know that someone had missed me. I scooped him into my arms.

"Is Bill here?" I asked Darcy.

She shook her head. "You just missed him. He brought Roger for me to keep while he runs errands."

"Was he alone?" As soon as I asked, I wished I could snatch the question back. I was acting like a jealous harpy. And with no reason. At least, I hoped I had no reason.

"He was by himself," Darcy said with a puzzled look. "And he didn't say where he was going."

I tried to act nonchalant. "Anything else going on?"

She handed me a pink slip. "A Mr. Moore called a few minutes ago."

I read the message written in Darcy's neat script. J.D. was currently at the Lassiters. I checked my watch. I could stop by the sisters' house on my way into Clearwater to talk to Adler, but confronting J.D. was a task I dreaded. I didn't know what I'd do if he was mentally ill, as I feared. If he presented a definite threat to himself or the Lassiter women, I could arrange to have him committed under the Baker Act. But I'd need some kind of proof, and too often that evidence didn't arise until a subject had hurt someone. Otherwise, as long as the Lassiters refused to file trespassing charges, my hands were tied. My only other recourse would be to track down J.D.'s family, as the Lassiters wished, and ask that a relative take charge and see that he received proper medical assessment and care.

I took Roger into my office, removed a bone marrow treat from the box I kept in my desk drawer and offered it as compensation for abandoning him, which I was about to do again.

I returned to reception and told Darcy my itinerary.

"Any message for Bill?" She was watching me closely as if aware of the tension I'd been trying to hide.

On days like these, I was almost tempted to give in and get a cell phone, but I have an aversion to technology, especially computers and cell phones. Darcy handled my computer work, which took care of one problem, but carrying a cell phone would create an intrusion into my life that I didn't want. The only good thing about no longer being a cop was not being electronically connected to the world with a radio and beeper. So far, that disconnect hadn't been a problem. I could usually find a landline if I needed one, and I checked in with the office often in case of emergencies. But sometimes, like today, I wished for that instant connection with Bill.

"When Bill comes back, give him Kimberly Ross's phone number. He can reach me there after five o'clock. I'll be pulling the night shift."

With a pat for Roger, whose forlorn look nipped at my conscience, I headed out the door.

I FOUND J.D. in the front yard of the Lassiter house, trimming shrubbery. He wasn't the wild-eyed, aging hippie with long oily hair pulled back in a ponytail, dirty ragged clothes and a body covered with bizarre tattoos that I'd expected. The man, who appeared only a handful of years older than Bill, had the gentle demeanor and clean-scrubbed look of an old-fashioned country doctor or a favorite parish priest.

His gray hair was neatly trimmed in a short, military cut, and his clothes were worn and mended but clean, except for the perspiration that soaked them from his exertion in the humid morning air. His smooth, tanned cheeks were testament to a recent shave and his brown eyes were clear and smiling.

"If you're looking for Violet and Bessie," he called when I got out of my car in their driveway, "they've gone for their walk."

I gazed up and down the sidewalk but saw no sign of the elderly sisters.

"On the trail," J.D. added. "They walk two miles every morning. That must be what keeps them young."

I crossed the lawn, still wet with dew in the shade. "Actually, I came to see you."

His friendly smile faded.

"The Lassiters asked me to," I added quickly. "They're concerned about you."

He sighed, hunched one shoulder and wiped his perspiring face on his sleeve. "Are you a social worker?"

"I'm a private investigator. Violet and Bessie want me to find your family."

J.D. turned his back on me and took a couple of angry whacks at the Turk's Cap hedge beneath the front windows. "I don't want to find my family," he said through gritted teeth.

"Wouldn't you like to know who you really are?"

"No."

"Why not?"

J.D. dropped the loppers to his side and pivoted to face me. His eyes were pools of misery and fear. "Because I have dreams. If they're from my former life, it's better for everyone if that man stays dead and buried."

CHAPTER 6

"What kind of dreams?" I asked J.D., thinking his sleeping visions might be a window into his state of mental health.

"Blood. Death. Killing." He grimaced and shook his head. "I don't understand the nightmares. I'm not that kind of man. Not now, at least. I can't stand the thought of hurting anyone. That's why I want to leave the past behind. Things could be buried there I don't want to unearth."

Everyone had nightmares at one time or another. Bad dreams didn't automatically brand a person as crazy or homicidal, and J.D. appeared calm and caring. But I'd feel a lot better about the Lassiter sisters' safety if I knew more about J.D.'s past.

"How long have you been like this," I asked, "without your memories?"

The air was thick with moisture and mosquitoes and no breeze to alleviate, either. My blouse stuck to my skin, and sweat trickled into my eyes. I swatted mosquitoes with one hand and wiped my face with the other. Maybe J.D., who hadn't responded, thought I'd become uncomfortable enough to leave him alone, but, if so, he underestimated my persistence.

"How far back do you remember?" I said.

"You have no right to pry into my past." His voice held more frustration than belligerence. "I don't have to answer your questions."

"Yes, you do, because I'm concerned about two elderly sisters who have opened their home to a man they know nothing about. I need to be convinced that they're safe, that you're no threat to them. Either you deal with me, or I take my concerns to the sheriff's office. Which will it be?"

"I'd never hurt Violet or Bessie," he insisted with a stricken expression.

"Are you sure?"

"They've been good to me. Why would I hurt them?"

"Do you ever have blackouts? Hear voices?"

He shook his head and regarded me with a kindly smile that reminded me of my late father. "And I don't drink or do drugs, either. Believe me, Miss—"

"Skerritt. But you can call me Maggie." I felt drawn to J.D. in spite of my intention to remain objective.

He nodded. "Except for loss of memory and occasional night terrors, I'm as sane as you are. If I thought

I was a danger to Violet and Bessie or anyone else, I'd turn myself in."

"Then what's the harm in letting me run your prints to find out who you are?"

J.D. sighed. "My memory goes back only as far as July. One morning I awoke and found myself on the Pinellas Trail in Palm Harbor with no money, no identification, a blinding headache and no recollection of anything before that."

"Why didn't you go to the authorities?"

"I know it sounds foolish, but I'd had those dreams before I came to, and I was afraid I'd...done something I shouldn't have."

He was warming to his topic, so I didn't interrupt.

"For days, weeks, I scrounged old newspapers, looking for stories about missing persons. Or some horrible crime. If I had family worried about me, wouldn't they have contacted the press?"

"Maybe. Did you come to the Lassiters then?"

"Not at first. I stayed in homeless shelters in Tarpon Springs and Clearwater, but the people who ran them asked too many questions. Eventually I found an old bike someone had left as garbage on a curb. I fixed the chain and appropriated it for transportation. Between collecting cans and doing odd jobs, I earned enough money to buy food. I shopped in thrift stores for clothes. All I needed was a place to stay. That's when I discovered the toolshed out back, here. It's handy for my bike, being next to the Trail, and I worked out an exchange with Violet and Bessie, odd jobs in place of rent."

I found myself liking J.D. more by the minute. He seemed straightforward, honest, uncomplicated and my instincts were telling me he wasn't a threat. Nonetheless, I wanted to know who he was and what had happened to him. Just in case.

"Living in that shed violates zoning ordinances," I told him. "You could get the Lassiter sisters fined if you're discovered."

"I wouldn't want that," he said quickly. "They're already having a hard time financially."

"They do without a lot." I pointed to their open windows. "Air-conditioning, telephone, sometimes even food."

"But I'm not costing them anything. And I try to help them as much as I can."

"You don't belong on the street, J.D. I can tell by your speech that you're an intelligent, educated man. If you let me fingerprint you, we can solve the mystery of who you are. Whether you go back to your old life will be up to you."

"What if I don't have a choice?"

"You think you're in trouble with the law?"

"There's the rub," he said with a self-effacing smile. "I don't know if I am or not. But just from talking with you, I know that if I am, you'd be the first to turn me in."

What could I say? He had me pegged.

"Think about letting me run your prints." But I wouldn't leave the decision to him. I'd ask the Lassiter sisters to find something that J.D. had handled. My gut told me he was harmless, but I couldn't leave the safety of Violet and Bessie to a gastrointestinal hunch.

"Nice talking with you, Maggie," he said pleasantly and returned to his pruning to end the conversation.

I got into my car, turned the air on full blast and headed toward Clearwater.

I'D GONE ONLY a few blocks when the brief blare of a siren cut off midwail caught my attention. In the rearview mirror, I spotted a flashing red light on the dash of a white, unmarked car. I pulled to the curb, stopped and rolled down my window.

The white sedan parked behind me, and the driver's door opened. I watched in the side mirror as a tall, handsome man in khaki slacks and a knit shirt climbed out and approached my vehicle. With his dark hair, studly build and designer sunglasses, he could have been Tom Selleck's body double in the star's younger days.

But a handsome jackass is still a jackass. I resisted the urge to groan and slump down in my seat. I was in no mood for Detective Garrett Keating of the sheriff's office. Bill and I had solved a murder last June, and Keating had claimed the credit, in spite of the fact that he'd originally arrested the wrong person, our client, and had refused to believe in her innocence until we'd rubbed his nose in the facts of the case.

"I wasn't speeding," I declared when he reached my window.

He leaned forward and folded his muscular arms on the window frame. "Didn't say you were."

"You stop me for a reason or should I file a harassment complaint?"

"Maggie—" his breath, smelling of peppermint, brushed my cheek "—is that any way to greet an old friend?"

"Old friend? How about acquaintance of three months?"

"But I feel like I've known you forever."

His tired line might have worked on other women, but it made me want to gag. "I'm in a hurry. Some of us have to work for a living."

He ignored my barb. Or it went over his head. "Actually, I did stop you for a reason."

He was grinning like an idiot, and I'd moved as far away from him as my seat belt allowed. In the presence of Keating and his ego, I always felt crowded.

"I wanted to ask you to have dinner with me," he said.

I sighed. "We've been through this before. I'm engaged, Keating. You're wasting your time."

"Oh." Disappointment registered on his Magnum-look-alike face. "I thought that had changed."

"You thought *what* had changed?"

He shrugged his broad shoulders, and the movement produced a corresponding ripple in his impressive biceps. "I saw Malcolm last night going into Sophia's with a good-looking redhead, so I assumed—"

"You assumed wrong." So Bill had taken Trish to Sophia's, the most la-di-da restaurant in Pelican Bay? The green-eyed monster nipped at me, and I didn't mean the ex-wife. "We have a friend visiting from out of town. I'd have been with Bill and her, but we're working a 24-7 security detail and I drew duty last night."

My excuse sounded flimsy, even to me, but the problems of Bill's ex-wife were none of Keating's business. I was having a hard enough time avoiding the determined deputy without giving him the slightest whiff of hope that my relationship with Bill was rocky.

His grin widened, as if he'd guessed there was trouble in paradise. "Then maybe you'll have dinner with me when it's Malcolm's turn to work."

"Why would I do that?" I asked with feigned innocence.

"Because a pretty woman like you shouldn't eat alone," Keating said in a voice hot enough to melt wax.

"Sorry, got to run. I'm late for an appointment." I rolled up my window, forcing him to move his arms or have them pinched by the glass.

Leaving Keating standing in the street, watching me with his hands on his hips, I pulled away from the curb.

CHAPTER 7

When I arrived at the Clearwater Police Department, the parking lot was almost full, and more people than usual were coming and going from the downtown station. After showing my ID, I was admitted to the building and took the elevator to the criminal investigation department on the second floor. The room was packed with detectives, and I wondered if the city was experiencing a crime spree.

"What's going on?" I asked Adler.

"They just activated the Emergency Operations Center fifteen minutes ago." He waved me to a chair beside his desk and polished off what looked like the last of a Danish pastry. "You haven't seen this morning's weather forecast?"

I shook my head.

"Tropical Storm Harriet's been upgraded to a Category Two hurricane. It's gaining strength and forward speed and headed this way. The EOC is gearing up for evacuations. We'll all be pulling overtime until this blows over."

The county's Emergency Operations Center would have its hands full. Evacuating tens of thousands from the barrier islands over a handful of bridges, several of which were undergoing repairs and construction, was a daunting and probably impossible task. I thought immediately of Kimberly Ross in her high-rise.

"Can I use a phone?" I asked.

Adler pointed to the only empty desk in the room. I hurried to it, picked up the handset and dialed the penthouse. Mackley answered.

"We've got hurricane warnings," I said. "If you and Kimberly don't get off the beach now, you could be stuck in traffic before this thing hits."

"You want me to take her to my house?" he asked.

"Has FedEx delivered the letters from her Omaha office?"

"They arrived a few minutes ago."

"Pack them with Kimberly's things and move her to my condo. You can get the key from Darcy at the office."

"Your place is in an evacuation zone, too."

"I'll take her somewhere from there later," I said. "At least you'll both be off the beach."

The somewhere later I had in mind was the house Bill and I had bought that was farther inland than my condo and fitted with impact-resistant windows and shutters. But I didn't relish the idea of being cooped up with Trish. Bill's ex-wife was disaster enough without adding a natural one.

"Just get out of there as quickly as you can," I told Mackley. "I'll give you a call after you've reached my place."

"Will do. I'll check the weather. If this thing's moving fast, I'll have to cut my shift short so I can get home and put up shutters."

"No problem."

If Mackley had to return to Tampa before the bridges and causeways into Hillsborough County closed due to winds and flooding, I'd take over guarding Kimberly so he'd have time to reach home safely. If the Big One hit Pinellas County with high storm surge, forecasters had predicted that the entire peninsula would become two small islands, cut off from the rest of the state, with its roads and causeways underwater, its bridges destroyed.

I didn't have to warn Mackley to be careful leaving the building with Kimberly. If she had been the intended target, the shooter knew from the morning news that he'd missed her and had hit Sister Mary

Theresa instead. He could be lying in wait outside the building. But Abe knew his job. He'd create a diversion or give Kimberly a disguise. Or both.

After hanging up with Mackley, I called Darcy and asked her to make sure Bill knew about the storm. Under normal circumstances, he stayed on top of the weather, but with Trish to deal with, his situation was far from ordinary. I wanted to make certain he had time to secure the *Ten-Ninety-Eight* against the coming blow.

"Shut down the office now if you need to go home and make preparations," I told her.

I returned to the chair by Adler's desk. He looked harried and distracted, and his tousled sandy hair made him appear more boyish than ever.

"We're all on duty here till the storm passes," he said.

I understood the drill. The Emergency Operations Center called in all county and municipal employees to deal with the event, including evacuation, the storm's duration and its aftermath. Unlike the city of New Orleans prior to Katrina, our county had a well-thought-out plan and the means to implement it and deal with the disaster. Transportation, shelters and evacuation procedures were in place, and residents had been repeatedly warned since the first of April to have at least three days of supplies ready, because they might be on their own at least that long if a hurricane swept our part of the state.

"I need a favor, Maggie," Adler said.

"You've got it," I replied without hesitation. Adler had provided invaluable help in many of my investigations. I owed him. And I loved him like the son I'd never had. All he had to do was ask.

"I don't want Sharon and Jessica alone during the storm. There's a shelter for employees' families, but it will be crowded with people who live in evacuation zones. My girls will be more comfortable at home, as long as someone's with them."

I'd been planning to take Kimberly with me to Bill's and my house, a few blocks from the Adlers, but Adler's request gave me an out from having to endure the hurricane confined with Trish. The original drama queen, who fainted over a hangnail, she'd be a raging lunatic during a real emergency.

"Any problem with my bringing Kimberly Ross to your house, too?" I asked.

Adler shook his head. "Sharon will appreciate the company and moral support."

Sharon, six months pregnant with their second child, and almost-two-year-old Jessica, were the lights of Adler's life. "I'll take good care of her and Jessica," I promised.

"Hey, Maggie." Ralph Porter left the fax machine on the other side of the room and joined us with a fistful of papers. Tall and skinny with an Elvis-style pompadour, jeans, short sleeves, string tie and drawling Southern twang to his speech, Ralph's hayseed look often misled people into underestimating his abilities. I called it the Columbo syndrome. But, like Alder, Ralph was a first-rate detective. "What brings you here?"

"Our agency's protecting Kimberly Ross. She's convinced she was supposed to be the target in the Sand Key shooting yesterday. Much as I appreciate the billable hours, I'm hoping you can prove she's wrong."

Porter and Adler exchanged glances.

"You know she's Wynona Wisdom?" Porter asked.

I nodded.

Adler picked up a large plastic evidence bag that contained a section of newspaper and handed it to me. "We found this in the hotel room used by the shooter."

"No other evidence was left behind," Porter said, "so we believe the shooter placed it there on purpose."

"In the trash?" I asked.

Adler shook his head. "It was lying on top of the spread in the middle of a bed that hadn't been slept in."

"Any prints?"

"None on the newspaper."

"In the room?"

"Oh, yeah. Tons of prints and DNA." Porter made a face. "You know how it is with a hotel or motel room, in spite of the fact that this is a high-class joint that's cleaned thoroughly every day. It'll take the crime lab weeks to sort through and identify the evidence."

I could read the newspaper print through the clear plastic. The section was from the *Washington Post* a few weeks ago and was folded back to reveal that edition's "Ask Wynona Wisdom" column, which contained three letters and Wynona's answers.

"This can't be coincidence," I said with a sigh. "Looks as if Kimberly's right. She was the target."

Adler shook his head. "Not necessarily. Read the second letter."

I scanned the text. The letter writer described how her teenage daughter had committed suicide after being barred from a women's health center by protesters. The eighteen-year-old had attempted, but failed, to cross the picket lines to receive counseling concerning an unexpected and unwanted pregnancy. The mother was asking Wynona's advice on how to deal with her anger and grief. Wynona's answer was compassionate and practical, suggesting grief therapy and support groups.

"What's your point?" I asked Adler when I'd finished reading. "Isn't Wynona still the obvious target?"

"We did a background investigation on Sister Mary Theresa," he said.

"She wasn't a member of a contemplative order," Porter explained. "She was an activist who spent most of her time organizing peaceful pro-life demonstrations at women's clinics around the country."

"So you think Wynona, aka Kimberly, wasn't the intended victim," I asked, "but someone out for revenge against the nun for their daughter's suicide?"

"It's possible," Adler said. "We can't be certain that the nun protested at whichever clinic was referred to in the letter on that particular day. We'll have to do some more digging. Wynona's staff is trying to run down the original letter to see if it's postmarked or gives some other indication of what city the writer lived in."

"Like *Sleepless in Seattle*," I said, "only Grief-stricken in Galveston?"

"If we're lucky," Adler continued. "Often the letters are edited for length and clarity, so the original may provide more clues than what's in the paper."

"The D.C. paper left in the hotel could point to the shooter's city of origin," Ralph said.

"Or be a red herring to throw us off track," I said. "With her high public profile, Sister Mary Theresa could have attracted the attention—and animosity—of any number of nutcases around the country."

"Maybe," Adler said. "Read the third letter in the column."

I read. The writer was another distraught woman, this one the wife of a physically abusive husband who was currently serving time for crimes unrelated to spouse abuse. He was due for release soon, and the woman, who had no means to support herself and her small children, had asked Wynona what she should do. Wynona had replied emphatically that the woman should contact the nearest shelter and arrange to relocate and to change her name, if necessary, before her husband was released.

I glanced up at Adler when I'd finished reading. "So Kimberly could have been right after all, if the shooter was the ex-con, who blamed Wynona for the disappearance of his wife and children and was itching to settle a score."

"Kimberly's staff is searching for the original of this woman's letter, too," Adler said.

"What's your guess?" Porter asked me.

I glanced at the third letter in the column left by the shooter. It was a request for Wynona's meat loaf recipe, which she'd provided. Even if the meat loaf wasn't to everyone's taste, I doubted it was grounds for murder.

The more I knew, the less I knew. "It's a toss-up. Until we do a lot more investigating, we won't know whether the shooter was after Wynona or the nun."

My job for now was to keep Kimberly Ross alive until we could find whether the answer lay behind Door Number One or Door Number Two.

CHAPTER 8

"These might help." Porter waved the sheaf of papers still clutched in his fist. "Ballistics report on the bullet that killed the nun. Mick Rafferty just faxed it from the crime lab."

Adler took the report and scanned it. "The rifling from the bullet indicates it was fired from a Model 70 Winchester bolt-action rifle, .308 caliber."

I sighed. "A gun commonly used for hunting. Sheer numbers will make it harder to trace. The shot was fired from a good distance. That means our shooter needed some expertise. A former military or law-enforcement sniper, maybe?"

"Could be," Porter said with a nod. "But a Bushnell scope with automatic ranging could have compensated for lack of skill."

"Under normal circumstances," Adler said, "if this storm wasn't bearing down, we'd start canvassing area gun shops to check for recent sales of that model rifle."

"If the shooter's from out of the area," I said, "he could have brought it with him. And if he's our ex-con, he had to get it on the black market, since it's illegal for him to own a firearm."

"Or he could have bought it from an individual instead of a dealer," Porter said, "so a background check wouldn't have been required and there's no paperwork in the system."

"Or our shooter could have faked his identity to buy the gun," Adler added. "We know he checked into the hotel under a false name and address."

"License number?" I asked.

"A Florida tag, also faked when he registered," Adler said. "Nothing like it listed with DMV. And we're fairly certain he wasn't foolish enough to give the real make and model of his car on the room registration. A hotel with that many rooms doesn't have time to verify all information."

"So the only thing we know for sure is that the shooter was male?" I asked.

"Even that's not certain." Adler tugged at his earlobe, a familiar gesture. "Tomorrow's Friday, the beginning of Labor Day weekend. The hotel was already jammed when the shooter checked in. None of the staff remembers that particular guest with any clarity, so we have no physical description. He registered as

James Johnson, but 'he' could have been a woman in a clever disguise."

"A rifle isn't usually a woman's weapon of choice," Porter said.

"Unless you're Annie Oakley," I said.

The murder investigation was grinding to a halt as much from lack of solid information as the distractions and demands of the approaching hurricane, and my arms and face were itching like mad. A glance in a mirror would probably confirm that my antihomicidal hives had returned with a vengeance.

"If Kimberly actually was the intended victim," I added, "living in a gated community twenty stories up, she'd be hard to hit any way other than a long-range shot."

Adler combed his fingers through his hair. "We're getting nowhere, and with Harriet barreling toward us, we may have to put our investigation on hold until the storm passes."

"Kimberly's staff FedExed boxes of death threats she's received," I said. "Mackley's bringing them to my place when he and Kimberly evacuate the beach. Kimberly and I can sort through them while we wait out the storm at your house, Adler."

He nodded. "Sharon can help. Maybe you'll come up with something."

"Did Kimberly tell you about her ex-fiancé?" I asked.

Porter and Adler exchanged glances, then shook their heads.

"He came up in conversation last night. Seems he was so controlling Kimberly moved from Omaha to Florida to escape."

"Name?" Adler asked.

"Simon Anderson, an investment counselor in Omaha."

Adler made a note in the file. "We'll check him out."

"I'd better go," I said, "and let you guys get to work."

"Stay safe," Adler said.

"You, too." I glanced toward the ceiling-mounted television set in the far corner of the room. A satellite picture of Harriet, with a visible eye and swirling bands of cloud cover that spread from Mexico across Cuba, was lumbering through the Yucatan straits on a projected course toward Tampa Bay.

Staying safe had suddenly become a whole lot harder.

ON MY WAY BACK to my office, I stopped once again at the Lassiter house, only two blocks from the waterfront and in an evacuation zone.

J.D. was nowhere in sight. I parked in the driveway and knocked at the front door. Violet answered.

Behind her, Bessie was gathering pillows, blankets and collapsible lawn chairs and placing them beside a canvas carryall that appeared filled with canned goods and file folders. Just inside the front entrance stood two small, square overnight bags, circa 1950.

"Do you need a lift to a shelter?" I asked.

"That's very kind of you," Violet said, "but Mr. Moore next door is driving us to JFK Middle School in Clearwater. It's the nearest shelter. We're leaving soon to be sure they'll have space for us. His family will be staying with friends who live near the school."

"What about J.D.?" I asked.

Bessie had joined Violet at the door. "He took off on his bike after he heard the forecast. Said not to worry about him, that he'd take refuge somewhere."

"But we do worry about him." Violet's voice, usually firm and assertive, trembled, reflecting her fears and her advanced age. "We worry about everyone."

I understood her concern. After several hurricane seasons with the most numerous and intense storms on record, everyone in the state was suffering from hurricane fatigue and probably at least a mild form of post-traumatic stress disorder due to the constant battering from the life-threatening and unpredictable storms. And Pelican Bay, which hadn't taken a direct hit, had merely endured the anxiety of close calls. I couldn't begin to imagine what people in devastated areas had suffered. With Harriet lumbering our way like a doomsday machine, we all hoped for the best and prepared for the worst.

For the elderly, like Violet and Bessie, who made up such a high percentage of the area's population, the stress of evacuating and riding out even near misses had to take its toll.

"I'll check with you when the storm's passed," I said. "When this is all over, if you can locate something with J.D.'s fingerprints, I might be able to identify him for you."

If Harriet didn't blow everything away.

"If he comes back," Bessie said.

"I'm sure he'll find a safe place to ride out the storm," I said.

Violet shook her head. "That's not what Bessie means. J.D. said you'd talked with him. He was upset. We don't know if he'll come back at all."

Her tone was accusatory, as if I'd run him off.

"For now," I said, "you need to concentrate on taking care of yourselves. If J.D. doesn't come back after the storm, I'll try to find him."

But my promise was an empty one. If Harriet hit the Bay area with the force predicted, hundreds of thousands would be displaced and homeless, and finding J.D. would be the least of our worries.

DARCY WAS BATTENING down the office when I arrived. Roger greeted me in a frenzy of barking, jumping and turning in circles. He'd picked up on our anxiety over the approaching storm.

"Bill wanted to leave Roger here while he secured his boat." Darcy took a stack of folders from her desk, shoved them into the nearest file cabinet and locked the drawer. She waved toward the other rooms with their tall sash windows overlooking Main Street. "Better take anything you don't want to lose. Those windows have no shutters, and that wavy old glass will break the first time any wind-driven debris hits it."

"Will you ride this out at home?" I asked.

She shook her head. "I'll put up my shutters, then go to Mama's. Her house is on higher ground, and I don't want her alone during the storm. You'll be with Bill at the new house?"

I shook my head. "Adler asked me to stay with Sharon and Jessica. And I'll take Kimberly Ross, our new client, with us. Go on home and secure your house. There's nothing more to do here."

She opened her desk drawer, removed her purse and slung its strap over her shoulder. She wrote hurriedly on a desk pad, ripped off the sheet and handed it to me. "Here's Mama's address and phone, in case you need to reach me after the storm."

"You have Adler's home number?"

She nodded. Neither of us mentioned the probability that all phone service would be knocked out by the storm, even cell phones, whose towers would be demolished by high winds.

Her dark eyes filled with worry. "Take care, Maggie."

"You, too."

She patted Roger, then hurried out.

I went into my office, picked up the phone and dialed my mother's house.

Estelle, Mother's elderly housekeeper, answered. "Your mama's already gone."

"Where?"

"She and Miss Caroline and Mr. Hunt flew to New York City earlier this morning. They're going to shop for clothes for the Queen of Hearts ball next February."

I should have known. Shopping was my sister Caroline's remedy for everything. And if she had to evacuate, what better place than the shopping mecca of Fifth Avenue?

"You aren't staying at the house?" I asked. The home where I'd grown up was a waterfront estate, susceptible to both strong winds and storm surge.

"Don't you worry 'bout me, Miss Margaret. My nephew, the doctor, is coming from Pasco County in a few minutes to take me home with him. I'll be fine."

"That's good."

"Where you gonna be?"

"At the Adlers, friends who live over a mile from the waterfront."

My throat closed with unwanted emotion. With a storm threatening, my own mother hadn't bothered to check with me to make sure I'd be safe. But I shouldn't have expected her concern. As a continual embarrassment and disappointment to my social-climbing parent, I was certain the less she thought about me, the happier she was.

"You and your Mr. Malcolm take care of each other, you hear?" Estelle had been more of a mother to me than my own. I could hear the love in her voice, which made me feel better.

"We will. You stay safe, Estelle."

I returned the receiver to its cradle and scanned the office. The only thing of irreplaceable value was Roger, so I hooked his leash to his collar, led him out and locked the door, not knowing if the building, a block from St. Joseph Sound, would still be standing once the storm had passed.

I HAD ONE STOP to make before returning to my condo. Unable to handle my ambivalent feelings about the return of Trish, I'd been avoiding Bill. But with disaster looming, I had to see him, to tell him I loved him.

When I reached his boat slip, the *Ten-Ninety-Eight* was already secured with extra lines and bumpers. Having gone through this drill before, I knew the precautions would protect the boat in a near miss, but a direct hit would wash boats, docks and everything else in its path inland. Some hearty mariners rode out storms onboard, and some even lived to tell about it, but Bill was more cautious, for which I was thankful. He could buy a new boat, but I could never replace him.

With a packed duffel bag slung over his shoulder, he was locking the slider to his cabin when I approached.

"Looking for a good time, sailor?"

He sprang from the deck to the dock, dropped the duffel and picked me up in a bear hug that almost crushed my ribs.

"God, I've missed you."

"It hasn't been that long," I protested, but his enthusiasm was reassuring. And Trish was nowhere in sight.

"Are you packed?" he asked when he released me.

"In a manner of speaking. My emergency gear is ready to put in the car."

"Good. Then I'll meet you at the house?"

I shook my head. "Adler asked me to stay with Sharon and Jessica. He doesn't want them alone during the storm."

He nodded and, to my relief, seemed obviously disappointed.

"Will you and Trish be okay?" I said.

"It's going to be a long haul." He frowned. "On top of her breakup, this storm is sending Trish over the edge. She won't stop crying."

In my experience, female histrionics did one of two things to a man: sent him running in the opposite direction or evoked a comforting response. As empathetic as Bill was, he'd try to ease Trish's pain. And I didn't want to picture where that might lead. For a moment I wanted to go with Bill to act as a buffer between him and the emotional tug of his ex-wife. But I'd promised Adler, and I also had to trust Bill. If his love wasn't strong enough to weather this temptation, I needed to know before I married him.

"At least you'll only be a couple of blocks away,"

he said. "That's good to know. I'll come and check on you when the worst is over."

When the worst was over.

But no one really knew how bad it was going to be.

CHAPTER 9

Mackley was pacing in my living room when I arrived at the condo. Kimberly stood at the sliding glass door, watching the waters of the bay, which were almost as smooth as glass.

The calm before the storm is a cliché but also a truth. The approaching monster Harriet had sucked the moisture from the air, leaving the sky a flawless, cloudless blue, the temperature pleasant and the air amazingly dry for a tropical summer day. Not a single cloud or any other hint of the coming fury dotted the horizon.

"I've got to leave, Maggie," Mackley said when I entered the room. "The damned thing's been upgraded to a Category Three, moving toward us at twenty miles an hour. The National Hurricane Center thinks it will be a Cat Five by the time it hits."

"I'll take over here," I said. "Be careful, Abe. Check in after this passes and let us know that you're all right."

He hurried out, and Kimberly turned from the sliders. I'd kept Roger on his leash.

"I hope you like dogs," I said.

She smiled. "Love 'em, but the condo association won't let us have pets."

"Mine didn't, either, until I petitioned for an exception. It was granted only because I'll be moving out soon. In the meantime, Roger makes one false move and we're both evicted."

I unhooked his lead and he bounded to greet our guest. Weeks of training had paid off, because Roger didn't go for her legs. His humping habit had finally been broken. Kimberly kneeled and scooped him into her arms. He reciprocated by washing her face with his tongue.

"Sorry," I said, "Roger can't hold his licker."

"Don't worry. No matter how bad things are, a dog can always make me feel better."

"Any trouble leaving the condo?"

She set Roger down and shook her head. "We were lost in the shuffle. Residents were loading their cars, preparing to evacuate. And Abe had me dress in the extra set of clothes he'd brought with him and stuff my hair under a ball cap. Since we left in Abe's car, even if the shooter was watching, he wouldn't have spotted me."

I glanced back to the hall, where Kimberly's boxes and luggage were piled.

"I brought my own hurricane kit," she said, "with extra water and food."

Knowing Kimberly's propensity to chow down when anxious, I was glad for the additional supplies. Before Harriet was through with us, anxiety was only the initial stage of an emotional scale that ran all the way past oh-my-God to scared spitless.

She jerked her thumb toward the water behind her. "We're not staying here?"

"We're sheltering with the Adlers, a mile or so east of here."

"Adler, the detective?"

"His wife and daughter. Dave has to work."

"On finding Sister Mary Theresa's killer, I hope?"

"Not until the storm blows over. The entire department will be tied up with evacuations and emergency calls. And after that?" I shrugged. Who knew what any of us would face once Harriet was through with us. "You brought the hate mail?"

She pointed toward two FedEx cartons stacked in the hall.

"We'll take them with us," I said. "Sharon, Dave's wife, will help us go through them."

I didn't add that having work was a good thing, to keep us from going crazy as the storm approached.

FOR THE NEXT FIVE hours, we were too busy to be worried. Kimberly helped load her supplies and mine, along with Roger's doggie lounger, into my Volvo. Protecting the windows and sliders on my condo involved no more than the flip of switches, and the electrically powered shutters lowered and locked.

When we reached the Adler house, preparations became more complicated and more frenzied. Sharon, a short, slender dynamo with light brown hair and a frazzled look in her hazel eyes, had thawed and was cooking most of the food from her freezer in anticipation of power outages. Jessica, sensing the tension, missing her daddy and upset by her altered routine, cried and clung to her mother's legs. Not even Roger's playful presence consoled her.

While Sharon juggled toddler and roasted beef, Kimberly and I shifted lawn furniture and trash cans into the garage before tackling the window coverings.

The neighborhood was strangely deserted. Most people were either already cloistered in their shuttered homes or had taken a chance on avoiding gridlock and evacuated, even though the EOC had repeatedly begged that those not in actual evacuation zones ride out the storm at home to avoid being snarled in traffic when Harriet hit. Only a few last-minute souls, like us, were clearing loose objects from their patios and lawns and rushing to put up window protection.

I could hear the sound of hammering down the street. Someone was nailing plywood to window openings. He might as well have covered his glass with plastic wrap. One good tug of wind would rip nails out of a building and turn sheets of plywood into deadly flying missiles. Lots of long screws at frequent intervals to hold the wood were the best insurance against the wind breaching the inside of a house. For months, newspapers and television news reports had carried computerized models that showed roofs lifting and walls collapsing once hurricane winds entered buildings through improperly secured windows or garage doors. The possibilities for disaster were endless and terrifying. No wonder so many had hit the road to try to outrun the storm.

At the Adler house, the coverings for the French doors across the back of the family room, like my condo shutters, were electronic. As long as we lowered them before losing power, we could take advantage of the daylight and save ourselves a few hours of claustrophobia. The rest of the house had sash windows with permanently installed tracks and bolts for mounting corrugated aluminum shutters and fastening them in place with wing nuts.

I learned the hard way that the shutters had jagged cutting edges, but once I'd applied a few Band-Aids and borrowed a pair of Adler's work gloves, I was in business. Kimberly and I formed an assembly line. I inserted a shutter panel into the track and she provided the wing nuts to lock them.

She handed me one of the shiny fasteners.

"Not the kind of nuts you usually work with," I said.

I hoped some humor would alleviate the strain that was visibly building inside her. In spite of the sticky heat, her face had lost its color, and her fingers, when she passed me a fastener, trembled. She'd been through the wringer the past two days, shocked by Sister Mary Theresa's murder, fearful she'd been the intended target, knowing that her condo stood like a huge bull's-eye in the path of a killer storm and that she remained in the hurricane's crosshairs, as well. I wasn't big on medication, but I was beginning to wish I had a stash of Xanax to help Kimberly make it through the night. If my favorite meteorologists were on the money, our situation was only going to get a whole lot worse.

On the other hand, Sharon was cooking enough food to feed a platoon, so Kimberly just might have enough culinary anesthesia.

"You ladies need some help?" a familiar voice sounded behind me.

I shoved the aluminum panel I was holding on to the protruding bolts and turned around. "Kimberly, meet Bill Malcolm, my partner in Pelican Bay Investigations."

"Hi," Kimberly said. "Have you come to stay with us?"

Bill shook his head. "Our house is two blocks over. I'll be keeping an eye on it during the storm." He took the bag of wing nuts from her. "Why don't you get something cold to drink? You'll dehydrate fast in this heat."

Kimberly, smart enough to sense that Bill wanted to talk to me alone, went inside.

"What's up?" I asked.

"Besides Trish's hysteria?" Bill made a face. "She's in bad shape. She was already an emotional wreck from Harvey's desertion. Now she's blaming me for putting her in harm's way."

"That's the Trish I remember." I felt guilty satisfaction at her irrational behavior, which was setting Bill's teeth on edge. Her bad, my gain.

"She wants to evacuate to Georgia," he added.

"You might have time to make it out of the county before the bridges close."

"And leave you here? I'd be a basket case, worrying about you." His expression turned grim. "This could be really bad, Margaret."

"I know." I'd seen the devastation of previous storms with killer surges that had scoured the earth inland for a mile and a half. And if Harriet came at us from a certain angle, we'd face not only an assault of towering water from the Gulf but from Tampa Bay, as well, an aquatic pincer move.

Bill reached to the tree beside him, hefted an ax he'd leaned there and handed it to me. "Adler has a pull-down ladder to his attic. If the water rises, you can use this to hack through the roof."

I felt the blood drain from my face.

"Just think of it as extra backup that you probably won't need," he said with a reassuring smile.

"If I have your ax, what will you do?"

"I have a gasoline-powered chain saw, but I'm hoping I don't have to cut a hole in our new roof before we've even moved in."

I nodded.

"Now," his voice was all business, "you handle the wing nuts while I get the rest of these panels mounted."

"Will Trish be okay alone for now?"

"She'll have to be. Besides, you need some help, and I had to get away. Once we're buttoned down as the storm approaches, I can't escape. I don't want to prolong the agony of enduring her complaints."

FOR THE NEXT HOUR, Bill and I worked in companionable silence. By the time the aluminum shutters covered all the Adlers' windows, the sky had turned a leaden gray and the breeze had stiffened. Suddenly rain spattered, and we dashed to the front porch, now empty of its welcoming swing and chairs, pots of geraniums and Jessica's toys.

Bill gazed at the sky. "The first of the feeder bands has arrived. I'd better go."

He gathered me in his arms and kissed me until I couldn't breathe, then released me and sprinted down the walk. At the front gate, he turned, rain streaming down his face and shouted, "I love you, Margaret."

"I love you," I said.

I realized then how foolish my jealousy had been. At that moment, I didn't worry that Bill might fall in love with his ex-wife. I simply prayed that he and all of us survived the coming storm and that I would see him again.

CHAPTER 10

The sun wouldn't set for two hours, but daylight had become a moot point. A thick pall of clouds rotated in a semicircular band from the southeast, forerunners of the storm. Sharon had turned on the inside lights an hour ago. Battery-operated fluorescent lanterns stood at the ready, scattered throughout the house. Seasoned storm veterans, Sharon and I knew that the use of candles merely added another level of danger to an already perilous situation.

When I'd carried in the ax Bill had given me and placed it in the hall closet nearest the attic opening and out of Jessica's reach, Sharon hadn't commented, but I'd seen the shock in her eyes.

"Dave called while you were putting up shutters," she said. "They've made all traffic lanes off the Gulf beaches eastbound, but cars are still backed up all the way across the causeways. The police are working hard to get everyone off the roads and into shelters as soon as possible."

"Thank God I left when I did—" Kimberly turned a whiter shade of pale, and her eyes grew round behind her designer frames "—or I'd be stuck out there, too."

Exhausted by fussing and crying, Jessica, clutching her favorite stuffed lamb and sucking her thumb, had fallen asleep on the family-room rug. Sharon lifted her, took her into her bedroom and tucked her into her crib.

Sharon returned to the family room, where the French doors remained uncovered, and the outside lights illuminated shrubs and tree branches, twisted and tossed by the gusting winds. Fallen clumps of Spanish moss and a growing mat of twigs and small branches dotted the lawn. From the entertainment center, the television broadcast continual local weather coverage and satellite photos showed the massive storm inching northeast across the Gulf.

"All we can do now is wait," Sharon said.

According to the forecast, Harriet was hours away but maintaining her relentless advance toward Tampa Bay. The oven and refrigerator were filled with food, but none of us had an appetite, not even the usually ravenous Kimberly, whose anxiety had apparently passed a gastronomical tipping point.

"Let's tackle those boxes of letters," I said.

"Letters?" Sharon asked.

We had all been so preoccupied with preparations, I hadn't had a chance until now to explain anything to Sharon other than Kimberly's being a client who was sheltering with me. When Sharon learned that her guest was Wynona Wisdom, her jaw dropped.

"I read you every day. Your advice is awesome."

"And apparently deadly," Kimberly said with a forced smile.

But at Sharon's words of praise, Kimberly stopped staring out the window at the whiplashed branches, and a bit of her color returned.

Sharon pointed to the FedEx boxes I'd moved to the large farmhouse table in the eat-in kitchen. "Are those requests for advice?"

I shook my head. "They're mostly demands that Ms. Wisdom eat dirt and die."

I outlined briefly the facts of Sister Mary Theresa's murder and the reasons Kimberly feared she'd been the target. "If Wynona Wisdom *was* the intended victim," I concluded, "I'm hoping one of these letters will lead us to the shooter."

"Okay," Sharon said, "judging from the newspaper column left by the shooter in the hotel, we should look for any letters from a man whose wife left him on Wynona's advice?"

"Specifically if that man's writing from prison," Kimberly added. "I've counseled hundreds of women to get out of bad marriages. Letters from angry ex-husbands may be a common theme among the threats."

We sat around the table and I dug into the first box for a handful of letters for each of us. For several long minutes, the only sounds inside were the rustlings of papers and from outdoors the keening of wind through the trees. At one point, we all jumped when a broken branch clattered against the shutter on the kitchen window.

We shared nervous laughter and settled back to reading.

"Ewwwww," Sharon said with disgust after perusing the first few lines of a letter. She dangled it between her thumb and forefinger at arm's length toward Kimberly. "This one's a real sicko. A blow-by-blow description of your slow and painful death."

I took the letter. As a cop's wife, Sharon had been exposed to more details of mayhem and murder than the average woman, but she didn't need such graphic description, especially under the current harrowing circumstances. Neither did Kimberly.

"Any more like these," I said to both of them, "just place them in my stack and I'll read them."

I finished scanning the sadistic account but found no clue to the writer's background or what had set him off. The envelope was postmarked from a small town in Maine.

"He's probably not the gunman," Kimberly said. "Mary Theresa's death wasn't gruesome enough for his taste. Also, if that letter is similar to other slasher threats I've received, an analysis will reveal that this guy's too impotent to act on his fantasies."

The phone rang and Sharon picked up the portable handset beside her. "It's for you."

She handed me the phone. I took it and moved into the living room out of earshot of the others.

"Just checking in while the phone still works," Bill said. "Everything okay over there?"

"We're catching up on our correspondence. How about you?"

"Trish was climbing the walls, so I made a pitcher of margaritas. I can't believe she drank the whole thing. She's passed out on the sofa and should sleep through the storm. I only hope I don't have to carry her into the attic if the water rises. She's put on weight since the divorce."

"Which one? From you or Harvey?"

"Probably both."

God would get me, maybe before the storm was

over, but I silently celebrated Trish's extra pounds. She'd been entirely too beautiful in her early years and, although we'd both grown older, I welcomed any defects in Bill's ex-wife that leveled the current playing field.

"You been watching the weather?" Bill asked.

"Off and on."

"The latest report says the Bermuda High is starting to shift. If it slides south far enough and fast enough, it could steer the storm away from us."

"And if it doesn't?"

"Harriet will be a Cat Five with thirty-foot storm surge and one-hundred-and-eighty-mile-an-hour gusts when she hits."

I sighed. "Life in Pelican Bay didn't used to be so scary."

"Yes, it did. You grew up with Priscilla, remember?"

I laughed. Talking with Bill always made me feel better. "Speaking of Mother, she's with Caroline and Hunt in New York City. As far as my mother and sister are concerned, whoever said money can't buy happiness didn't know where to shop."

"I'll keep checking in as long as the phones work," Bill said. "Take care, Margaret. I miss you."

"I miss you, too."

I took the phone, joined Sharon and Kimberly

again at the table and pushed away thoughts of Bill and Trish alone in the intimacy of our house. I picked up the next letter from my stack and read through it.

"We can put God on our list of suspects," I said when I finished.

"You're kidding?" Sharon said.

I shook my head. "According to this woman, he's going to strike Wynona Wisdom dead because she advised the writer's middle-aged son to get a life of his own and not be a doormat for his elderly mother. Apparently, Wynona incited the son to break the Honor Thy Father And Mother commandment, and God is pissed."

As if on cue, lightning struck nearby with a concurrent crash of thunder.

"He sounds pissed," Kimberly said with a shudder.

Sharon took the next item from her stack. "Here's a letter from Pelican Bay," she said in surprise.

"Let me see." I took the letter, read it, then checked the return address on the envelope. "Wrong Pelican Bay. This is from the maximum security prison by the same name in California. This guy's angry, but he's also, if you can believe what he's written, serving a life sentence without parole."

I put the letter in the stack we'd designated for suspects.

Kimberly frowned. "Why save his letter? Didn't you say he's in prison for life? How could he be our shooter?"

"He can't," I said. "But he could have called in a favor from one of his friends on the outside. I'll check him out."

Another tree limb crashed into the house, this time against one of the French doors. Rain, driven sideways by the wind, sounded like scattershot when it hit the glass panes and the lights in the house flickered. At my feet beneath the table in his doggie lounger, Roger slept through it all. The only sounds my stalwart canine feared were vacuum cleaners and flying insects.

Sharon rose from her chair. "I'd better lower the rest of the shutters before we lose power."

She pushed a switch beside the wall of French doors and the panels slid down with a rumble, closing off our last outside view.

I wasn't usually claustrophobic. In my years with the Tampa PD, I'd worked in a windowless office. But this confinement was different. Not having visual access to the outside where the storm raged was nerveracking. The weather maps on television, the concussion of thunder, the impact of debris hitting the house and, most horrifying, the unrelenting howl of the wind were our only clues to what was happening around us. As the storm grew in ferocity, stepping outside to check would no longer be an option. Many people would dare either to satisfy their curiosity, videotape the catastrophe or face the storm's wrath rather than endure the suffocating claustrophobia. But those foolish enough to leave shelter would run the risk of being impaled by wind-driven debris, electrocuted by downed power lines or bitten by snakes or rats, driven from their burrows by rising water.

It was going to be a very long night.

Sharon came back into the kitchen from lowering the shutters in the family room. "We should get something to eat before—"

The explosion of a nearby transformer blasted over the roar of the wind; Kimberly uttered a high-pitched shriek, and the lights and television went off, plunging the house into total darkness without ambient light from outside to alleviate the pitch-black.

I fumbled for the fluorescent lantern on the tabletop beside me and turned it on. Sharon flicked on a similar light in the kitchen and carried it down the hall to check on Jessica. She returned a few seconds later.

"She must have worn herself out fussing. Not even the transformer blowing woke her."

In the sickly blue glow of the lantern, Kimberly looked anxious and ill.

"Maybe we should get something to eat," I said, "and take a break from these letters."

"Need some help?" Kimberly asked Sharon.

I caught Sharon's eye and nodded. Kimberly would fare better staying busy.

"Sure," Sharon said. "You can slice the roast for sandwiches while I toss a salad."

Kimberly went to the sink, washed her hands and started carving thin slices of beef off the roast Sharon had removed earlier from the oven. Sharon had turned on the battery-operated radio, where the television channels were broadcasting the latest storm coordinates for those who'd lost power. Harriet had moved up the coast, parallel to Naples, but was still offshore, still strengthening and still bearing toward Tampa Bay.

We were all scared. Fear hung in the room like a noxious cloud. Sharon switched off the radio. We'd all go crazy if we concentrated on every detail of Harriet's forward progress.

I fed Roger, clipped on his lead and took him through the attached garage to the side door. We stepped out under the eaves, protected from the wind that blew against the far side of the house, while

Roger did his business. When we returned inside, Sharon and Kimberly had shoved aside the piles of letters to set supper on the table.

With a nod toward Kimberly, Sharon said to me, "Maybe you should tell us some of your stupid criminal stories from your patrol days in Tampa."

Sharon had never been much of a talker, but she recognized the need to keep our minds off the storm. We took our seats again and I searched my memory for tales from my early days as Bill's partner, stories that would lighten the heavy atmosphere in the room.

"The stupidest criminals were the convenience store robbers," I said. "My first year on the force, a nineteen-year-old drug addict went into a store on Dale Mabry, plopped a twenty on the counter and asked for change. When the clerk opened the cash drawer, the robber pulled a gun and demanded all the money in the register. The clerk complied, the robber took the money and fled."

Kimberly looked at me, waiting for the punch line.

"He left his twenty on the counter," I said. "But there was less than twelve dollars in the cash drawer. Prosecutors were scratching their heads over that one. If a guy pulls a gun on you and gives you money, is it robbery?"

"You're making this up," Kimberly said, but at least

she was smiling and had lost her deer-in-the-head-lights look.

I shook my head. "It's on the record. As is the case of the beer thief. He stole two six-packs at knife-point. When the clerk accused him of not being old enough to drink, the guy was insulted. He pulled out his wallet and shoved his driver's license in the clerk's face to prove his age. The clerk memorized the name and address and we arrested the jerk at his house twenty minutes later."

For the next hour, I told stories while we ate and the wind and rain grew stronger. With supper finished, we returned to the letters. Another hour and our pile of suspect letters had barely grown. Most of the other written threats against Wynona Wisdom had been too vague or untraceable to be helpful.

The weather was deteriorating quickly. The breaks of calm between feeder bands lessened, the rain poured harder and the wind grew fiercer. We'd adjusted to the lack of light, but the hours without air-conditioning were taking a toll. The house was hot, stuffy and humid, making breathing more difficult and life in general miserable.

And it was going to get worse before it got better.

A blast of wind shook the house. Outside, a hor-rendous snap, like a giant stepping on a mammoth twig, sounded above the gale. A second later, a crash rocked the building. Roger leaped from his bed in a frenzy of barking, tangling in my legs as I pushed from the table.

With the sound of splintering wood and the house's shudder came a scream from Jessica's room.

Sharon grabbed a lantern and raced down the hallway. I took another lantern and followed.

We both stopped short in the doorway, unable to enter. The branches of a gigantic pine filled the baby's room, blocking our access to the crib.

CHAPTER 11

"Mommy, Mommy, want out!"

Rain poured through the yawning gap in the roof, and intruding wind shook the fallen branches of the pine.

"Mommy's coming, sweetie," Sharon called. She was trying without luck to climb through the tangle of tree limbs.

In the hall behind me, Kimberly was talking to the 9-1-1 operator on her cell phone. "Yes, I know there's a hurricane coming, but we have a toddler trapped in her bedroom by a fallen tree. We need help." She turned to me. "What's the address here?"

I gave her the street and number, then reached into the hall closet and grabbed the ax Bill had left. At the door of Jessica's room, I pulled Sharon by the arm. "Get out of my way. I'll try to cut through to her."

I hacked at a limb the size of my arm. Sweat and rain poured into my eyes, and the concussion from the ax caused the tree's needles to lash my face. The pungent odor of pine sap mixed with the smell of wet insulation and drywall had filled the room. With every blow of the ax, Jessica cried harder. I prayed her tears came from fright, not injuries. Sharon kept up a flow of reassurances in a futile effort to calm the child.

"Fire and rescue's on the way," Kimberly called out.

My muscles burned from their unaccustomed exertion, but Jessica's pitiful cries kept me going. When I'd cleaved the heavy limb, Kimberly, Sharon and I grabbed it to pull it aside, but its movement shifted the entire tree, dropping it a few inches farther into the room.

"Stop!" I yelled, afraid the trunk would crush the crib and Jessica with it. "We'll have to wait for the firefighters."

Sharon whimpered. She would have chewed through the branches with her teeth if she'd thought the action would get her closer to Jessica, but all she could do was talk to the little girl.

"Mommy's here," Sharon called in a calm voice at odds with the panic on her face. "As soon as the nice men come to take the tree out of your room, Mommy will come get you, sweetie."

Jessica screamed louder. So did the wind.

Then, above the strident duet of child and weather came the blessed sound of sirens.

"Thank God," Sharon murmured.

Kimberly, still connected to 9-1-1 on her cell, told the operator, "I can hear them coming."

"Tell the operator to alert the crews that the tree is shifting and might crush the child if it isn't braced," I told her.

Kimberly relayed the information. Sharon kept up her patter of words, and Jessica continued to cry. I looked around for Roger and found him huddled in his bed beneath the kitchen table.

Now the sound of engines and grinding gears joined the sirens as the rescue trucks approached. I ordered Roger to stay and went onto the porch as a line of vehicles pulled to a halt at the curb. A ladder truck, a paramedics van and another engine, lights flashing, killed their sirens, and men in turnout gear poured from the vehicles, their neon-yellow slickers shiny with rain in the pulsing emergency lights.

Joe Fenton, a paramedic I knew well from my days on PBPD, bounded onto the porch. I explained the life-threatening situation in Jessica's room.

"Is the kid injured?" he shouted above the wind.

"We can't get close enough to tell," I said, "but she's

still screaming her lungs out. I'm hoping that's a good sign."

He nodded, returned to the curb and filled in the supervisor on the scene. With calm but amazing swiftness, the rescue team, armed with jacks, pulleys and chain saws, attacked the monster pine from outside the house. Another pair brought more equipment inside and headed to Jessica's room.

Carrying their gear, Joe and his partner, a young woman I'd never met, went inside and waited for the rescuers to clear access to Jessica.

I went back inside, too, but Kimberly and I, knowing there was nothing we could do, stayed in the kitchen out of the way.

The whine of chain saws joined the howl of the wind and drowned out Jessica's cries. At least I hoped that was what had happened and that the little girl hadn't fallen silent from injuries.

"Your face is bleeding." Kimberly pointed to my right cheek.

I lifted my hand, sticky with sap, to my face, and it came away smeared with blood. "Must have been hit by a flying wood chip."

But the cut was inconsequential. All I cared about was what was happening in Jessica's room. I picked up Roger to keep him from getting underfoot or bounding out the open front door where firefighters came and went, and I sat down next to Kimberly at the kitchen table.

The firefighters were racing against both the approaching storm and the danger of the wind shifting the tree and causing it to fall and crush Jessica. I thought of Adler, protecting the citizens of Clearwater, unaware his only child was in mortal danger. I eyed Kimberly's cell phone, but decided notifying Adler now would be cruel. He'd risk his own life if he tried to return home, and being away and unable to help would drive him crazy.

In a strange juxtaposition of men and women working at full tilt to free Jessica, and the slow crawl of time, I waited. The high-pitched whine of chain saws ceased abruptly, voices shouted over the wind, and the floor of the house shook as the massive tree shifted and dropped.

I closed my eyes, not knowing if they'd reached Jessica in time and dreading the pain Sharon and Adler faced if they hadn't.

The torture of the unknown was short-lived. A cheer went up in Jessica's room, and a huge firefighter with tiny Jessica dwarfed in his burly arms strode into the family room with Sharon close behind.

The fireman handed the bawling child to Joe, and

the paramedic and his partner checked her out. Aside from a few scratches on her face and a throat most likely sore from overuse, the toddler was fine.

Hearing the verdict, Sharon collapsed into a chair and Joe placed Jessica in her arms. The child gripped her mother around the neck in a choke hold, and Sharon smiled through tears.

The paramedics packed up their gear, and the firefighter, Ferguson, according to the name on his turnout, announced, "We're putting a tarp over the damaged roof, but you can't stay here. The envelope of the house is compromised, and if the storm hits, the rest of the roof will go. We can move you to a shelter if we hurry."

I thought of the public shelters, already overcrowded, and weighed our options. "My house is two blocks over. Can you take us there?"

He nodded. "Get whatever stuff you need, but make it snappy."

"Is that okay with you, Sharon?" I asked.

"What?" She was still in shock, and my conversation with Ferguson hadn't registered.

I repeated what he'd said along with my suggestion to go to my house, and she nodded.

"My bins are still packed," I said.

"Mine, too," Kimberly said, "except for these boxes of letters."

"I'll hold Jessica," I offered to Sharon, "while you grab what you need. But we have to hurry."

Jessica came into my arms without protest. For some reason, the kid had always liked me from the day I'd met her at the party for her first birthday. Sharon disappeared down the hall to her bedroom and returned a few minutes later with a carryall.

The firefighters, obviously weary from spending the past forty-eight hours moving the elderly, handi-capped and special-needs citizens to shelters, helped take our bins and luggage to their truck. Kimberly toted the FedEx boxes, I picked up Roger and Sharon cradled Jessica in her arms. We dashed through the driving rain and fought against the wind to reach the rescue vehicles, where we all managed to squeeze inside. When we reached my house, I raced ahead of the others and banged on the front door.

Bill answered, and surprise registered on his face when he saw me and glanced past me to the fire truck.

"Is there any room at the inn?" I asked.

BILL'S SURPRISE HADN'T affected his reflexes. In a few short seconds, he'd assessed the situation and leaped into action to help the firefighters unload their pas-sengers and baggage. As soon as we were safely inside, the fire and rescue personnel piled onto their trucks and headed back to the station to ride out the storm or answer the next call, whichever came first.

Roger, delighted to be in familiar surroundings, raced through the living room straight to the sofa where Trish still slept and licked her face. Trish, lost in margaritaville throughout our arrival, awoke with a shriek and smacked Roger across the nose. The pug, who'd never had a voice or hand raised against him, yelped and retreated to the kitchen.

"You hit my dog again," I told her, "and you'll be weathering this storm outside."

"Do I know you?" Trish peered at me through bleary eyes, and her words were slurred.

"Maggie Skerritt, the other owner of this house."

I was being territorial, but I couldn't help it. After all we'd been through, I had one nerve left, and Trish was getting on it.

Ever the peacemaker, Bill jumped into what threatened to become a fray. "Why don't I take Trish to the guest room so she can go back to sleep? The rest of you make yourselves at home."

Bill helped the tipsy Trish to her feet. She looked as if she'd just crawled over forty miles of bad road. Her clothes were disheveled, her aging face blotched and puffy, her makeup smeared and her tangled red hair showed two inches of gray roots. In my mind's eye, I'd pictured Trish as she'd been twenty-three years ago, vibrant and beautiful. I'd have felt pity for the wreck before me now—if she hadn't hit my dog.

While Bill half-carried Trish to the guest room, I went into the kitchen and coaxed Roger from beneath the table with a bone marrow treat from the box we kept in the cabinet by the sink. The pooch was trembling from his ordeal, and I petted him and offered consoling words before carrying him back into the living room.

Bill had returned with an armload of blankets and pillows for Sharon. "We can make Jessica a pallet on the floor, if you like."

Sharon nodded. "I want to keep her close."

I filled Bill in on the tree's crashing through Jessica's room and causing our evacuation, and set Roger in his bed next to Jessica's pallet.

Bill caught my attention. "I closed the door to the guest room, so Roger can't get to Trish."

"Lucky for her." I was still angry at the woman who had struck a small, helpless animal. Drunkenness was no excuse. Trish's life had taken a bad turn, but I wouldn't allow her to take out her frustration on my dog.

Our house was a cozy oasis in the storm. The hardwood floors of the sixty-year-old Cape Cod gleamed, the perfect backdrop for the mission-style furniture Bill had inherited from his parents. In winter, the fireplace with its oak mantel would be a cheerful gathering point.

Only then did I notice that the lights, air-conditioning and television were working. "We still have power."

"So far," Bill said with a satisfied grin.

But my words had been a jinx. No sooner had Bill acknowledged them than the house plunged into darkness.

CHAPTER 12

Bill turned on a battery-operated lantern on the mantel, and the huge mirror hanging above it reflected its light back into the room.

Kimberly reached for the lantern she'd brought with her, but I shook my head. "Better save it. We could be days without power."

Bill hadn't drawn the curtains on the sash windows, unshuttered since they were impact-resistant glass, but the blackness of the storm prevented us from seeing what was happening outside.

Probably just as well. We were all shaken from Jessica's close call and the damage to the Adler house and all too aware that those incidents could be only the beginning of a series of events that would turn even more deadly as the storm drew nearer.

Bill disappeared down the hall and returned a few minutes later with a tiny battery-powered TV. He set it on the mantel beside the lantern and turned it on.

We watched and listened as Paul Dellegatto from

Channel 13 gave Harriet's latest coordinates and pro-jected path. Once the meteorologist's words sank in, we clapped and cheered.

"This calls for a celebration," Bill said. "Anyone for margaritas?"

"Good idea," I said, thinking of Trish, oblivious in the guest room. "Then we can all get some sleep."

HURRICANES ARE FICKLE and unpredictable, which must be why they're named after people. Harriet, after threatening and terrifying the population of Tampa Bay and initiating the most massive evacuation in the area's history, abruptly veered west off Sanibel, did a loop in the Gulf and headed for the coast of Mexico.

After a margarita-induced sleep, we awoke late the next morning, in shock from our near miss, with our moods swinging from elation to pangs of guilt that the catastrophe that had been meant for us would wreak havoc elsewhere.

Later that morning, after the worst of the wind had blown by, Sharon and Jessica returned to their damaged home, and Kimberly and I to my condo. Tens of thousands of other evacuees also headed home. They jammed roadways, caught in gridlock, and grumbled that they wouldn't leave next time because the storms never hit where predicted. They conveniently forgot that this same attitude had doomed thousands in New Orleans and along the Mississippi and Alabama coasts a few years earlier.

Shutters came down, power company trucks streamed into neighborhoods to restore blown transformers and downed lines and yard cleanups began. An unfortunate few, like the Adlers, whose homes had sustained damage, met with insurance adjusters and contractors for repair estimates.

A volunteer crew of off-duty officers from the Clearwater PD arrived at the Adlers that afternoon, armed with chain saws to remove the massive pine from Jessica's room and the side yard. Within hours, a stack of pine logs stood by the curb, awaiting removal by the city's sanitation trucks. A blue tarp was tacked firmly over the gaping hole in the roof. Adler moved Jessica's crib into the master bedroom until the roof was repaired and her room restored.

Rather than return to her Sand Key condo, Kimberly remained with me. Until we'd sorted out whether Sister Mary Theresa's killer had mistaken his victim, Kimberly no longer felt safe in her own home. With her computer, fax machine and forwarded phone lines, she settled into my spare room and resumed dispensing advice to millions of faithful readers.

At my insistence, not even her staff were told her new location. All mail and packages were sent in care of my office. With our new precautions in place, Kimberly felt safe enough to stay alone during the day with Roger as watchdog and companion, while I worked with Adler and Porter to sort out the mystery of the nun's death.

Bill usually helped on an investigation of this scope but, after a day of clearing Spanish moss and tree debris from the lawn of our house, he had been occupied with chauffeuring Trish to look at apartments and apply for jobs. Although we'd talked on the phone, I hadn't seen him in the week since the evacuation had ended. We met at the Dock of the Bay for dinner, and he sat across from me in our favorite booth.

"Where's your ball and chain?" I should have felt contrite for sounding petty, but I resented Trish's intrusion into our lives. Dealing with unpredictable hurricanes was bad enough. Ex-wives were an added annoyance.

"She's having dinner with old friends from Tampa," Bill said. "They picked her up at the house an hour ago."

The waitress came to take our drink orders.

"Draft beer," Bill said.

"I'll have the house water."

The waitress left and Bill cocked an eyebrow. "You on the wagon?"

"I'm still detoxing from your post-hurricane-party margaritas. What did you put in those things, knockout drops?"

He grinned. "They did the trick, didn't they? You, Sharon and Kimberly were wound tighter than a cheap watch when the firefighters dropped you off. But, thanks to a few stiff drinks, you all had a good night's sleep."

Trish, who'd consumed more of the power-punch than the rest of us, had still been sleeping when we'd left that morning. She'd been so blotto, I doubted she remembered my threats from the night before after she'd slapped Roger. Bill had suggested the three of us have dinner two nights ago, but I'd had no desire to make nice with the woman. The sooner she was out of our lives, the better.

"Any luck finding Trish an apartment?" I said.

"God knows, I've tried. The ones she likes, she can't afford. The ones she can afford she claims she's afraid to live in."

"Afraid?"

"She says they're filled with lowlifes and criminals." He shook his head. "Apparently, living with

Harvey honed her expensive taste. She has no idea what a lowlife, crime-ridden complex is like. The ones we've looked at are cream puffs in comparison."

A niggling little suspicion flowered in my brain. "Does she know about your inheritance?"

"When I told her Dad had passed away, she asked what would happen to his orange groves."

When Trish and Bill had been married, he'd earned only a cop's salary and his dad had been barely eking a living out of his groves. Now Bill owned real estate worth millions and no longer hit the streets to serve and protect every day. Combine that with his good looks and great personality, and what woman wouldn't want him? I wouldn't put it past Trish to try to win him back.

"How much longer will she be in our house?" I knew I sounded petulant, but didn't care. I wanted the woman gone. Yesterday.

"Why, Margaret—" His blue eyes twinkled. "I think you're jealous."

"I miss you."

"I miss you, too," he said. "When will your house guest be leaving?"

"Not any time soon. I met with Adler and Porter this afternoon. Porter spent the past two days in Boston, checking out Sister Mary Theresa's background. No one in the diocese knew of any threats against her. Everyone he spoke with said that she was well-loved and respected."

"But she was an activist?"

I nodded. "But apparently, a very peaceful and civilized one. The protesters she led were always nonconfrontational, obeyed the rules and never harassed anyone. Porter says he doubts the column in the newspaper the shooter left in the hotel room is related to the nun."

"Which leaves the ex-con whose wife left him on Wynona Wisdom's advice."

"Unless," I said, not entirely joking, "someone died from the meat loaf recipe."

The waitress arrived with our drinks, and I took a sip before continuing.

"We have a stack of threatening letters to Ms. Wisdom from inmates and ex-cons. Adler, Porter and I are working through them now, hoping to turn up a suspect."

"Any chance you could take next weekend off?"

"Maybe. If I can get Abe to stay nights at my condo with Kimberly. She's okay during the day, but freaks out when the sun sets. What do you have in mind?"

"Some R & R on the boat, a little cruise on the Intracoastal, a bit of fine dining, a lot of fooling around."

The prospect was enticing, especially the fooling around part. "What will you do with Trish?"

"I'm hoping she'll have found her own place by then."

"She'll need a car."

"I'll buy her a used one."

After the way Trish had taken Bill to the cleaners in their divorce settlement and deprived him of participating in his daughter's growing up, she didn't deserve such kind and generous treatment. But if Bill hadn't reached out to her as he had, he wouldn't be the man I'd come to love, so I kept my objections to myself.

"And what about a job?" I added.

"She reads the classifieds every day."

"But has she made any calls, scheduled any interviews?"

He shook his head. "She's either not qualified or not interested in any openings she's found."

Why should she be interested? my dark side muttered. She'd fallen into hog heaven, living in Bill's house with him carting her around, paying her bills, and providing for her every need.

"You can't support her forever," I said, in spite of my good intentions not to complain.

"She needs time."

"She needs to be self-sufficient. You're not helping

by letting her go from dependency on Harvey to dependency on you."

"That's a bit harsh."

"It's a harsh world. As ex-cops, we know that better than most people."

"So what harm does it do," he asked with irritating logic, "to make life easier for someone?"

Feeling whiny and small in light of Bill's generous nature, I shrugged. "None, I suppose."

The waitress returned to take our order, but my appetite had disappeared. I gave myself a silent pep talk, promising that by this time next week, Trish would be out of our lives, Bill and I would have our weekend and all would be right with the world.

I should have known better.

EARLY THE NEXT MORNING, remembering my promise to the Lassiter sisters, I drove to their house. Piles of tree branches and trash cans overflowing with leaves and Spanish moss lined the curb, but their yard was immaculate. I wondered if J.D. had returned for cleanup duty or if Mr. Moore next door had helped the elderly women. Their house showed no signs of damage from the storm's near miss.

Violet answered the door. "Miss Skerritt, come in."

I stepped into the small living room filled with

heavy Victorian furniture. Although the windows were open, air barely stirred inside the house, and the temperature seemed even warmer than outside, but Violet wore her usual cardigan.

"We could sit on the porch—" she had lowered her voice to a whisper "—but if you're here about J.D., he's working in the backyard and might overhear us."

She waved me to a seat on a high-backed settee, and Bessie came in.

"Bring us some iced tea," Violet ordered her sister.

Accepting her subservient role without protest, Bessie did an about-face to the kitchen, and Violet took the chair across from me.

"I hope the evacuation wasn't too hard on you," I said.

"Hard?" Violet laughed. "I can't remember when Bessie and I have had so much fun. The shelter volunteers prepared all our meals. And we met the most fascinating people, who'd also evacuated. One couple helped us make up a foursome, and we spent most of our time playing bridge. I'd forgotten how much I enjoy the game. I was almost sorry when we had to leave and come home."

Violet's positive attitude was probably a factor in her longevity. When life tossed her lemons, she made champagne.

"I didn't think J.D. would come back," she said, "but he was here when we returned from the shelter, already picking up the debris left by the storm."

I peered through the open back door and across the porch and spotted J.D. digging in the sunny backyard. "What's he doing now?"

"Preparing a vegetable garden," Violet said. "He really is the most thoughtful man. Says if he plants now, we may still have time to grow a winter crop."

I had to give J.D. credit. As strapped as the Lassiters were for income, fresh vegetables would be a welcome addition to their diet. But just because J.D. was behaving generously and responsibly now didn't mean he wouldn't snap sooner or later if he had a psychological problem that had caused his amnesia and put him on the streets. He could be a ticking time bomb right under two sweet old ladies' noses.

"I need your help," I said to Violet and Bessie, who'd come back from the kitchen with a tray filled with glasses of iced tea. "If I can have something with J.D.'s fingerprints, I'll see if there's a match in the national data bank."

"You think he's a criminal?" Violet asked in disbelief.

"The system holds more than fingerprints of criminals," I said. "Everyone who's been in the military, taught school, worked for the government or needed a security clearance has been fingerprinted."

Bessie placed the tray on the low table between Violet and me and picked up one of the glasses. "I'll be right back."

She hurried across the back porch and out into the yard. I watched as J.D. set aside his shovel, accepted the glass from Bessie and downed its contents in a few swallows. He returned the glass. Fortunately, he also resumed his digging, so he didn't notice Bessie holding the glass by the rim between her thumb and index finger to avoid smudging his prints.

"Do you have a plastic bag?" I asked Violet.

She went into the kitchen and returned with a grocery sack. When Bessie came in, I took the glass from her and wrapped it in the plastic.

"How soon will you know anything?" Bessie asked.

"Identifying the prints could take some time," I said. "I'll have to call in a favor from someone in law enforcement with access to the database, and they'll have to work it into their schedule. I'm sorry."

"Oh, don't be sorry," Violet said with a smile. "That will give J.D. time to get the garden planted before he goes home to his family."

Or back to the funny farm, I thought, but kept that possibility to myself.

CHAPTER 13

Carrying the plastic bag with the glass with J.D.'s prints, I left the Lassiter house. It was only 10:00 a.m., 7:00 a.m. Pacific time, too early to place a call to California to the warden at Pelican Bay prison to check out the inmate who'd written a letter with detailed threats to Wynona Wisdom. I considered taking the glass to Adler to have him run the prints, but between his damaged house and the current murder investigation, the poor guy didn't need the added chore.

Instead, I drove downtown to the sheriff's substation, parked in what had been my old space when the building had been the Pelican Bay Police Department and went inside. I asked for Detective Keating at the dispatch desk. The dispatcher buzzed Keating on the intercom and told him he had a visitor.

Within minutes, he was striding up the hall, looking as if he'd won the lottery.

"Hey, Maggie, changed your mind about that dinner?"

"You never give up, do you, Keating?"

"That's what makes me such an outstanding investigator."

"And humble, too."

The dispatcher, a thin young man with a bad case of acne, was watching us with interest.

"Could we continue this conversation in your office?" I asked.

Keating stood aside and waved me ahead of him and down the hall toward what had once been my office. The fact that the guy had squatting rights on my old territory was a major factor in the antagonism I felt toward him. But I wouldn't coax a favor out of him with bad attitude, so I flashed a smile when he offered me a chair. He took the one behind his desk.

"We really should get to know each other better," he said.

"Why? We have nothing in common, I'm already in a serious relationship and I'm at least fifteen years older than you."

His smile didn't dim. "I like older women."

"An Oedipus complex?"

He frowned briefly at what was obviously an unfamiliar reference. "We have lots in common."

"You and Oedipus?"

"You and me."

I shook my head.

"We're both in law enforcement," he said.

I had to give him points for tenacity. "I *was* in law enforcement. I'm in private practice now."

"We worked well together on the Grove Spirit House case."

Bill and I had worked together well. Keating had botched it, but I didn't want to antagonize him by saying so when I'd come begging. I tried to keep my tone reasonable. The last thing I wanted was to encourage his delusion that he and I had a future together.

"You don't know anything about me," I said. "My taste in music, my hobbies, what I like to do in my free time."

"But finding out would be so much fun."

I took a deep breath and prayed for patience. Apparently, the only thing to discourage Casanova Keating's amorous advances would be a two-by-four upside the head. But he couldn't help me if he was unconscious. I cut to the chase.

"I have clients," I said, "two elderly ladies who have a homeless man doing odd jobs for them."

I left out the part about J.D.'s living in their toolshed. With that knowledge, Keating, in accordance with zoning ordinances, would be forced to evict J.D.

"The guy has no memory, and I want to check him out, make sure he's no danger to the women."

"You want me to talk to him?" Keating asked.

"Been there, done that." I handed him the plastic bag with the glass. "I want you to run his prints. If you can come up with a name and last known address, I'll take it from there."

"So what's in it for me?" His grin was lecherous.

"The satisfaction that you've helped protect two lovely old ladies in your jurisdiction."

His expression sobered. Keating was a jerk, but even he saw the reasoning in my request. "I'll see what I can do." The leer returned. "Now, about that dinner?"

"You know I'm about to be married. What's the point?"

"Maybe I'll change your mind."

"And maybe several million illegal immigrants will stampede back over the border to Mexico." With an ego like his, Keating should run for office.

"Okay, what say we call it quid pro quo?"

I narrowed my eyes in distrust. "Call what quid pro quo?"

"I run your John Doe's prints. When I have the results, we'll meet for dinner, two professionals getting together to share information." He gave me his best

Tom Selleck smile, which on Selleck would have been disarmingly attractive. On Keating, it gave me the willies.

"What's the harm?" he said.

I started to protest. However, by agreeing to run the prints, Keating was doing me a favor. I could wait and ask Adler or even Mick Rafferty at the crime lab, but J.D. could go round the bend in the interim and harm the Lassiters, a possibility I wasn't willing to risk.

"On one condition," I said.

His grin was triumphant. "What's that?"

"I want these prints ASAP."

"You can count on it," Keating said in a crooning tone. "The sooner I have them, the sooner I have you."

"Two professionals meeting for dinner," I reminded him.

He nodded. "But you never know where it might lead."

Probably to a black eye and a knee to his groin, but aloud I said, "Call my office, please, when you have the results."

"Why don't you give me your cell number? I can reach you more quickly."

"Don't have one," I said with satisfaction and added avoiding annoying sheriff's detectives as another reason not to cave in to pressure and acquire a cell phone.

BACK AT THE CONDO, with Kimberly upstairs working on her computer in the spare room, I sat at the counter in my kitchen and placed a call to Pelican Bay State Prison, a super-max facility in northern California. Its housing of the state's most hardened criminals had been well-documented by the media, including a *Sixty Minutes* segment that should have scared any potential lawbreaker with half a brain into going straight. I was groping in the dark to identify the writer of the threats against Wynona Wisdom, since the letter with the prison's return address had been signed merely, "A Pelican Bay Inmate."

With the warden unavailable, my call was transferred to an assistant, who identified himself as Wayne Jackson. I told him who I was and explained the threatening letter.

"Was it handwritten?" Jackson had a soft, cultured voice, at odds with his harsh environment.

"Looks as if it came off a printer."

"Then it couldn't have come from the prison," Jackson said. "Our inmates don't have access to type-writers, computers or word processors. And we have a staff of investigators who monitor all written com-munication in and out of the complex. They wouldn't have allowed even a handwritten threat to slip past them."

"So you're saying it's a hoax." I picked up my pen to cross this suspect off the list.

"Not necessarily," Jackson said. "Unfortunately, inmates have found a way to circumvent our censorship and communication blackout. They write on tiny slips of paper and wrap them in protective coverings. The missives, called 'kites' or 'wilas,' are given to visitors, who hide them in body cavities before leaving the prison."

Talk about a yuck factor. Delivering someone a message via body cavity—I shuddered at the options—wasn't exactly caring enough to send the very best. "So an inmate could have transmitted instructions—" not to mention any number of diseases "—to someone on the outside to write and send a letter with the prison's return address?"

"It's possible." In his refined, educated tone, Jackson could have been discussing Proust instead of perversion. "Our prison population is obsessed with honor and respect within the various gangs. If Ms. Wisdom offended an incarcerated gang leader, members on the outside would be instructed to take care of her."

"Which gangs are you talking about?"

Jackson's sigh resonated through the handset. "Take your pick. We have the Nuestra Familia,

Mexican Mafia, Aryan Brotherhood, Black Guerillas and the Nazi Low Riders."

I shivered. "You're talking bad dudes."

"The worst, any of whom wouldn't hesitate at taking out a nationally syndicated columnist if he thought she'd shown him disrespect."

"Or the letter could be a hoax."

"There's no way to know for sure, is there?" He sounded convivial and upbeat. Maybe he hadn't been at the prison long.

I thanked him for his help and hung up.

Kimberly stood in the doorway, and I didn't know how long she'd been listening.

"Any luck?" she asked.

I shook my head. "Want some coffee?"

She nodded. "I'm ready for a break."

I poured her a mug from the carafe warming on the coffeemaker's hot plate. "You need to get out, breathe some fresh air. You've been cooped up in here for days."

She shuddered. "Not as long as somebody out there is gunning for me."

"We don't know that. It's still possible the shooter was after the nun or firing at a random target."

She drank her coffee and cocked her head, as if in thought. "What about my column left in the room?"

"Coincidence. It was an entire section of newspaper, after all. With your advice syndicated in hundreds of major papers, the chance of your column being in any random section is high."

She stared at me, her wide eyes magnified by the lenses of her glasses. "You think I'm being paranoid."

I shook my head. "I think you're being cautious. Adler and Porter are checking out the other threatening letters, and the Omaha police are interviewing Simon Anderson. Maybe something will turn up."

"And if it doesn't?"

"You go back to your life. You can't hide forever."

"Great," she said with a bitter laugh, "and when someone finally kills me, I'll be dead right."

Decades on the job had honed my instincts. Something about Sister Mary Theresa's murder had me believing that she hadn't been the target, nor that hers had been a random killing. Kimberly was somehow involved, but I couldn't make the pieces fit.

"Tell me about your staff," I said.

"What do you want to know?" She scooted onto the bar stool next to mine.

"How long have they been with you?"

"Steve and Cindy have worked for me since I first went into syndication. All the others have been there at least five years."

"And they're all happy with their jobs?"

"Happy and well compensated with good pay and great benefits. Steve, for example, is taking his four weeks' vacation now. The others have similar employment packages. I believe in rewarding people for a job well done."

"Have you ever fired anyone?"

"I've had people resign for various reasons. Going back to school for a degree, a husband with a job transfer, maternity leave. But I've never—"

I could almost hear the synapses firing her memory.

She frowned. "I forgot about Tonya McClain."

I scribbled the name on my suspect list. "You fired her?"

"She was my fact-checker. Her job was to vet every column, make sure any facts I included were accurate."

"And she slipped up?"

"No, she was actually the best I ever had. I've never found anyone as good." Kimberly scratched the top of her head, digging her square white nails into her frizzy hair. "But she was...difficult."

"*Difficult* covers a lot of bases. Did she drink, miss work, raid the petty cash?"

"No, Tonya would never break a rule. But once she settled into her job, she started giving me grief about every column I wrote. She'd question my advice and suggest alternatives. At first, I would teasingly remind her that the column was Ask Wynona Wisdom, not Ask Tonya McClain, hoping to make my point gently."

"It didn't work?"

"Some people don't respond well to correction," Kimberly said.

I thought of Garrett Keating. "So what happened?"

"She became more and more confrontational. I didn't need the stress, so I canned her."

"And she didn't take it well?"

Kimberly shrugged. "She wasn't happy, but she didn't threaten me. In fact, she apologized and said she couldn't help being the way she was. Being in charge had been ingrained in her during her previous career."

"What did she do before working for you?"

"She was a career officer in the Army."

CHAPTER 14

"So…" I summarized my conversation with Kimberly to Adler and Porter at their desks at the Clearwater PD later that afternoon "…Ms. Wisdom fired an employee who'd been an Army officer."

"Weapons training is a given," Porter said.

"But Kimberly insisted the parting was amicable?" Adler asked.

I nodded. "And I struck out trying to locate the Pelican Bay inmate who sent the threatening letter. I did, however, narrow the list of senders down to five major gangs operating in California and elsewhere. That's only several thousand potential killers, give or take a few."

Adler sighed, tossed his pencil onto his desktop and laced his fingers behind his head. "This is a wild goose chase. Except for the ex-boyfriend, Simon Anderson, and Tonya McClain, we have no named suspects."

"Did the crime lab lift any usable prints from the hotel room?" I asked.

Porter shook his head. "We're spinning our wheels. We don't even know for sure that anyone's really after Wynona Wisdom."

"Until he makes another attempt," I said.

"Which," Adler pointed out, "he's not likely to do, since he doesn't know where she is."

"And she's still afraid to go home," I said.

The phone on Adler's desk rang, and he answered. He listened for several minutes, thanked the caller and hung up.

"That was a detective with the Omaha police department," he said. "They've located Kimberly's old boyfriend. Simon Anderson has been in Monte Carlo for the past three weeks. He gave the name of a prominent Omaha socialite he's traveling with as his alibi."

"What's the female equivalent of a sugar daddy?" Porter asked.

Adler glanced at me. "Probably not anything we could mention in mixed company."

"Now we're down to only one named suspect," I said, "and that's Tonya McClain. I'd suggest that Kimberly quit wasting her money on protection and go home, but something tells me we haven't heard the last of our shooter."

"Wynona Wisdom has buckets of money," Porter said. "Who gets it if she dies?"

I'd already covered that base with Kimberly. "A shelter for abused women in Omaha, AIDS research, and the Nature Conservancy."

"None of those organizations is likely to hire a hit man in order to speed up their inheritance," Adler said.

"So what do we do next?" Porter asked.

"Besides checking out McClain?" Adler said. "There's nothing else to do but wait."

I RETURNED TO MY OFFICE. Darcy met me with a handful of message slips and an inquisitive stare.

"When are you going to tell me what's going on?" she asked.

"I'm investigating a murder." I knew what she was asking, but I didn't want to talk about it.

Darcy's curiosity had apparently passed its tolerance point. She followed me into my office and plopped into the chair across from my desk as if staking a claim.

"Bill hasn't been into the office since before Hurricane Harriet," she said. "Did you two have a fight?"

I sank into my desk chair and shook my head.

"Is he out of town on assignment?"

"No."

"Then where is he? And don't tell me it's none of

my business," Darcy said. "If you and Malcolm split, this agency is toast and so is my job. That makes it my business."

Darcy was more than an employee. She was a friend and, although she hadn't openly stated it, concern for more than her job was obvious in her expression.

"Bill's with his ex-wife," I said.

Darcy's dark eyes mirrored her surprise. "Holy crap, Maggie, that's a bummer."

"It's not as bad as it sounds." Since my investigation was temporarily dead in the water, I took the time to fill Darcy in on the story of Bill's marriage and divorce and Trish's recent abandonment by her husband. "As a result, Bill's been helping Trish find an apartment and a job."

"Here?"

"Where else?"

"She should have gone to her daughter's."

"Melanie's a spoiled brat. She wouldn't have her."

"You have to get that woman out of your house, Maggie, while you still can."

"I trust Bill."

"This isn't about him. It's about her and what she's capable of. I know Trish's type. I see 'em all the time, women who think they're incomplete without a man to lean on. They play weak and helpless, and before some clueless guy knows what hit him, they have their claws sunk so deep he can't escape."

"Bill's not clueless," I said, hoping I was right.

Darcy shook her head and gave me a sad little smile. "He's a man, isn't he? That makes him vulnerable to a woman who makes him think he's her only hope, her savior. And especially if he loved Trish before. I'm telling you, Maggie, this woman is bad news."

"I can't just kick her out."

"Sure you can. It's your house, too."

"But if Bill's feeling sorry for her, my lack of sympathy will make him think I'm awful."

"Lordy, if he's that far gone, then it's already too late."

I was beginning to fear Darcy was right. Bill was in over his head, Trish was setting down roots and my putting my foot down would only make waves.

Then a brilliant idea hit me, and I smiled.

Darcy tilted her head and narrowed her eyes. "I know that look. What are you scheming?"

"I can't protest without looking bitchy, so what if I use reverse psychology?"

"You're not going to encourage Bill to spend more time with his ex? That could backfire."

"Uh-uh. I'm going to volunteer to help."

Comprehension dawned on Darcy's face in the form of an evil grin. "Trish won't know what hit her."

I nodded. "I'll ask Bill to take up the slack in the investigation, while I go apartment shopping and job hunting with Trish. Her poor-me act won't work on me."

"And you'll get her away from Bill. Good plan."

Darcy had grown up in a poor neighborhood, but with hard work, education and determination, she'd moved up and out.

"How'd you get to be so smart?" I said.

She shrugged. "When I was in high school, too many girls my age thought it was cool to get pregnant, have lots of babies. They hooked up with any dude who came along and ended up with a houseful of kids, all the bills and men who came and went when it suited them. I swore I'd never tie my self-esteem to a man."

"Is that why you've never married?"

A smile lighted her attractive face. "Don't get me wrong. I like men, but I don't need them. There's a difference. If the right man comes along, one who wants to be an equal partner, bear his share of the load, like your Bill, I'd marry in a heartbeat."

The phone rang, and Darcy reached across my desk to answer. "Pelican Bay Investigations."

She listened for a minute. "Yeah, Adler, she's right here."

Darcy handed me the receiver and returned to her office.

"What's up?" I asked.

"Tonya McClain," Adler said. "You'll never guess where we located her."

"Must be close or you wouldn't sound so interested."

"She's working as a civilian for CENTCOM at MacDill Air Force Base and living in a condo in Safety Harbor."

"This could be our lucky break," I said.

"I'll interview her tomorrow," Adler said. "I'd go tonight, but I have another meeting with the contractor. Sharon wants me to light a fire under him. And Porter's got a union meeting."

"I'll go," I said. "Give me the address."

Dave provided directions to Tonya's place off Philippe Parkway, and I jotted them down.

"This could be another dead end," he added.

"Maybe." But to me, the interview with Tonya was also a means to an end.

I hung up with Adler and punched in Bill's cell number.

"Where are you?" I asked when he answered.

"On my way to the house. I'm picking up Trish for dinner."

"Something's come up that I need you to do." I explained that Adler wanted someone to interview Tonya McClain as soon as possible.

"I'll get on it right after I take Trish to eat," Bill said.

"I have a better idea. Why don't I have dinner with Trish? She could probably use a woman's point of view on her situation. You'll have a break from chauffeur duty and a chance to get up to speed on our current investigation."

His instant agreement was gratifying. I gave him Tonya's address. "Tell Trish I'll pick her up in ten minutes."

Darcy was shutting down her computer when I came out of my office.

"Bill's going on an interview, and I'm taking Trish to dinner. It's about time I staked out my territory."

Darcy grinned. "The ex-Mrs. Malcolm won't know what hit her."

We exchanged high fives, and I left.

HAVING ANOTHER WOMAN answer the door at my own house was disconcerting. It also reinforced my resolve. Trish had been through a rough time, a traumatic and humiliating experience, and I sympathized with her, but her distress didn't give her the right to move in on my life. I needed to make that fact clear before she settled into thinking of Bill and all that came with him, sans me, as the solution to her current dilemma.

Her appearance had improved since the last time I saw her. Her face was no longer splotchy, her makeup was perfectly applied, and her hair, the seductive red of decades ago, no longer sported gray roots. She wore shorts, a knit top and flip-flops. Besides the few extra pounds, she still had her figure, but she looked her age. Tiny lines flared at the corners of her eyes and gave a crepe effect to her neck. But in spite of the inroads of time, she retained the blatant sexual appeal that had made the men of the Tampa PD drool with envy when she'd been married to Bill.

"You ready to go eat?" I said.

"I'm not dressed for going out. I'll wait until Bill gets back from his interview."

"That could be after midnight."

She raised well-plucked eyebrows in surprise. "But it's only five-fifteen."

"He'll be meeting with the Clearwater police and me to fill us in on what he found out about our current case. He'll probably pick up a sandwich coming back from Safety Harbor. I doubt you'll see him before tomorrow."

She pursed her mouth in disappointment. "You're sure?"

All's fair in love and war. I was lying through my teeth, but I nodded. "And what you're wearing is fine for where we're going."

"I don't like fast food."

"No Mickey Ds. I'm taking you to Bill's and my favorite place."

I could tell she was trying to think of an excuse, but she finally gave in. "Let me get my purse."

FIFTEEN MINUTES LATER, Trish and I walked into the foyer of the Dock of the Bay.

"Hey, Maggie," the hostess said. "Haven't seen you in a while. Where's Bill?"

"Working tonight. Is our booth available?"

The hostess grabbed a couple of menus and led us into the main dining room. From the old Wurlitzer in the corner, Dolly Parton was belting out "Here You Come Again."

Sliding into the booth, Trish made a face. "I hate country music."

Score one for the home team. "Bill and I like it. That's one reason we come here."

Trish looked around at the pine-paneled walls, draped with fishnets filled with shells and starfish, and turned up her nose. "Looks like a dive."

"They serve the best burgers in the county, the old-fashioned kind."

Trish made another face and flipped open her menu. "I don't eat red meat. Do they serve sushi?"

"Only if it's deep-fried."

The waitress appeared to take our drink orders. I asked for iced tea.

"I'll have iced tea, too," Trish said. "Long Island."

She must have seen the concern on my face.

"What's the problem?" she said when the waitress left. "You're the designated driver."

"You don't want to get too mellow. You still have shopping to do."

"No, I don't."

I nodded. "We're going to Publix after we eat so you can stock the kitchen."

Trish shook her head. "There's no need. I have coffee and stuff for sandwiches. Bill takes me out to eat."

"That's the problem," I said. "Bill doesn't have time."

"He hasn't complained."

I faked my sweetest smile. "He wouldn't, would he? He's such a sweetheart. But the pace is wearing on him. He's not as young as he used to be."

Since lightning hadn't struck me yet for telling whoppers, I continued. "In fact, he's asked me to give him a break."

Trish's face lighted. "You mean from seeing you?"

"Good heavens, no." I packed as much self-satisfaction into my laughter as it would hold. "He's complaining because he doesn't see me enough. I told him I'd take you on your errands tonight and tomorrow."

She eyed me with suspicion. "What will Bill be doing tomorrow?"

"Besides working? Getting the boat ready for our cruise next weekend."

Trish leaned back in her seat and crossed her arms over her chest. Her once-impressive bosom had yielded to gravity. "He didn't say anything to me about a cruise."

"No," I said airily. "Why would he? But now you see why getting the house stocked with groceries is important. Come this weekend, neither Bill nor I will be here to take you out to eat."

The waitress brought our drinks. Trish downed half of hers before ordering a chef's salad. I ordered broiled grouper.

"So," I said when the waitress departed, "you must miss Seattle."

"I try not to think about it." Her tone was more belligerent than sad.

I understood her anger. In her place, I'd be wishing Harvey and his new trophy wife slow and painful deaths and for Seattle to slide into the Pacific.

"You must have some good friends you'd like to see back home."

"Most of my friends are married. Now I'm a fifth wheel."

"What about Melanie?"

"Melanie has her own life."

"So does Bill."

"What's that supposed to mean?" She was apparently going for huffy, but after slugging back her entire drink, her slurring words dulled the effect.

"We're getting married in a few weeks." I showed her my engagement ring. "And we'll be moving into the house—which we bought together," I said with emphasis. "We'll need you out before then. That's why I'm taking you to look at apartments tomorrow. I'll start moving into our house as soon as we return from our cruise."

She had chugged the rest of her drink and motioned to the waitress to bring another. Trish's smile was sly and slightly drunken. "Maybe there won't be a wedding."

Now her cards were on the table. Her agenda was exactly as I'd feared. With Harvey out of the picture, she wanted Bill back.

"Give it up," I told her. "You don't have a chance."

The waitress brought another Long Island iced tea, and Trish drank greedily. At this rate, she wouldn't need an apartment. She'd need rehab.

She wiped her lips with the back of her hand, smearing lipstick across her cheek. "Bill loved me once. We were together for ten years. I gave him his only child."

A part of me felt compassion. Another part wanted to tear out her auburn tresses by their dyed roots. "And you took his child away. You divorced him, remember, and remarried."

She leaned across the table, so close I could smell the liquor on her breath. "But that old spark's still there. I can get him back."

Her claim shook me. I knew Bill loved me. God knows, he'd pursued me long and hard over the past two decades. But I also knew how much he'd loved Trish, and that knowledge stirred my old insecurities. But I didn't dare let Trish see me sweat. She'd move in like a shark at the scent of blood in the water.

"Maybe *you* still have the spark," I said. "Or maybe you just need a place to crash and burn after the mess you've made of your life. But Bill has moved on, and he hasn't looked back."

The waitress brought our food, but Trish didn't touch hers. She finished off her second drink and requested a third. If she felt so confident about a future with Bill, I doubted she'd be drowning her problems in booze. When the waitress took Trish's order to the bar, Bud, the bartender, caught my eye with a questioning look. Trish was already too drunk to grocery shop, so I nodded my agreement to refilling her glass.

"You should eat," I said to her. "You'll need your strength in the morning."

She stared at me with bleary eyes. "Why?"

"Because we're going to look for another place for you to live."

She wagged her head from side to side like a bobble doll. "Don't need one. Got Bill's."

"That's only temporary."

"He's gonna marry me."

The woman was three sheets to the wind, oblivious to reason or reality. I finished my grouper in silence while she nursed her third drink.

After I'd paid the check, Bud left the bar and the two of us half carried Trish to my Volvo. She gazed across the parking lot to the boat-filled marina. "Nothing but friggin' boats," she said drunkenly, "and fish stink."

"That's Pelican Bay," I said. "A quaint little drinking village with a fishing problem."

I opened the passenger door, Bud deposited Trish on the front seat and, after a commiserating look, returned to the restaurant. I fastened Trish's seat belt.

"Li'l Maggie Skerritt," she crooned in a slurring voice. "You were always too pretty. Didn't like you spendin' the days workin' with my husband. He didn't want a woman partner. Did he ever tell you that?"

"More times than I care to remember." When I'd been assigned to patrol on the Tampa PD, Bill had been certain having a female partner was going to get him killed. Until the day I'd saved his life.

I tucked her right arm across her lap, shut the door and rounded the car. Once inside, I started the engine and headed for the house, praying I'd get Trish home before she tossed her cookies in the front seat.

CHAPTER 15

Bill was waiting at my condo when I returned from dropping off Trish. He took me into his arms, kissed me and then stepped back and wrinkled his nose.

"Trish barfed all over our living room," I said. "I've spent the last hour cleaning up."

I stooped to pet Roger, who'd been begging for my attention.

"Is she ill?" Bill said.

"No, but she will be in the morning."

He nodded in comprehension. "She's been hitting the sauce hard since Harvey left."

"Maybe longer than that. Ever consider that her drinking might have been a factor in the split?"

Bill looked thoughtful.

"Why don't you make coffee," I said, "while I take a shower? Then you can tell me what you found out about Tonya McClain." I suddenly remembered I had a house guest. "Where's Kimberly?"

"She turned in about fifteen minutes ago. She seemed beat. The stress is taking its toll."

Roger followed me upstairs and lay across the entrance to the shower while I bathed and washed my hair. He watched me towel off, dry my hair and don my robe, then trotted downstairs behind me. The pooch gave a whole new meaning to showering with a friend.

The aroma of fresh-brewed coffee filled the living room, and Bill handed me a full mug.

"Decaf, three sugars, just the way you like it." He sat on the sofa and patted the cushion next to him.

"Thanks. I think I'll marry you."

"I'm counting on it. How about tomorrow?"

I settled beside him, and Roger, after trying unsuccessfully to squeeze between us, turned around three times before lying next to me. "Let's get Trish settled first."

"How did your girl-talk go tonight?" Bill said.

"Before it was cut short by the falling hammer of three Long Island iced teas? In a nutshell, Trish intends to win you back, kick me out and live together with you happily ever after."

Bill cursed and almost spilled his coffee. At the string of expletives, Roger dived off the sofa and under the coffee table.

"I hope you set her straight," Bill said.

"She didn't want to be confused with the facts. You're her great white hope."

Bill leaned back against the cushions and closed his eyes. "Another case of the rescuer becoming the victim."

His reaction was reassuring, but didn't solve our problem. "So what now?"

He opened his eyes and stared into mine. "I think it's time Trish paid a visit to Melanie. But from what you tell me, getting her out of the house will take some strong persuasion."

"I'd suggest dynamite, but it's so messy."

"Ah, Margaret," he said in that warm, deep voice that melted my bones, "you're such a good sport. Any other woman would have been throwing hissy fits from the get-go. You're one in a million."

I smiled. I'd thrown my hissy fits in private. If Bill wanted to believe I possessed stellar qualities, who was I to disillusion him? "We'll deal with Trish later. Tell me about Tonya."

Roger, sensing the tension had left the room, peeked from beneath the table and hopped onto the sofa again.

Bill drank his coffee, as if collecting his thoughts before he spoke. "McClain is an interesting woman. Mid-forties, typical spit-and-polish ex-military and very butch."

"So she wasn't asked and didn't tell?"

"Apparently."

"Did she have an alibi for the day of the shooting?"

Bill shook his head. "She says she was driving to Key West for a long Labor Day weekend, but didn't have a witness to back up her story."

"No credit card receipts for gas?"

"Claims she paid cash."

"So she could have traveled to Key West via Sand Key," I said. "It's maybe sixty miles out of the way."

"I don't know. Tonya was hard to read. She appeared surprised to learn that Kimberly is living in the Bay area."

"Does she own a rifle?" I asked.

Bill shrugged. "I asked, but she said that was none of my business, and if the police want to know, they can get a search warrant, if they have grounds."

"A suspicious attitude."

"Or very Second Amendment," he said. "I wouldn't want a detective, private or otherwise, sniffing into my business without cause."

"What did she say about being fired?"

"She insists that Kimberly's letting her go from the Wynona Wisdom staff was strictly over creative differences with no hard feelings."

"And you believed her?"

"She seemed convincing," he said. "But if she's a sociopath, she could smile and smile and still a villain be."

"I love it when you talk Shakespeare."

He wiggled his eyebrows. "You should hear me talk dirty."

I covered Roger's ears. "He's only a pup."

Bill sighed. "And you have a houseguest. And so do I." His expression brightened. "There's always the boat."

"Sorry," I said. "Kimberly's paying us not to leave her alone at night."

"That's irrational," Bill said. "Sister Mary Theresa was killed in broad daylight."

"Fear is rarely rational."

He nodded. "We still don't know for certain whether Kimberly's fear has a basis in fact. The woman can't spend the rest of her life looking over her shoulder."

"Maybe in a week or two, after the trauma of the shooting has lessened, she'll feel safe at home."

"Who's working this weekend while we're off on our cruise?" he asked.

"I've already lined up Mackley to spend the nights here."

He set aside his coffee and pulled me into his arms.

"We'll be married in a couple of weeks. How about a preview of coming attractions?"

AN EARLY RISER, I was at my desk at the office by eight the next morning, reading the classifieds and circling prospective apartments. I'd give Trish enough time to sleep off last night's excesses before taking her house hunting.

After lining up agents to show the properties and planning a route that would have Trish screaming to sign a lease, any lease, just to stop me from dragging her all over Upper Pinellas County, I turned to my notes on Kimberly's case.

So far, there was no prime suspect in Sister Mary Theresa's death. Forget prime. We didn't have even a secondary suspect, unless I counted Tonya McClain. Bill was returning to Tampa this morning to interview Tonya's neighbors and friends in hopes of turning up a current link between Tonya and her ex-boss. Meanwhile, the only connection between the nun's death and Kimberly was the physical resemblance between the two women. None of the threatening letters to Wynona Wisdom had panned out. No identifiable suspect with a grudge against the sister or Kimberly had surfaced and, if the sniper had been a random killer, he hadn't struck again, at least not in the Bay area.

My investigation had hit a wall. Unfortunately, in situations like this, often someone else had to die before the conundrum could be solved. That conclusion made my skin itch, and I reached into my desk for a Benadryl capsule to ward off homicide hives and washed it down with coffee.

The phone rang, and seconds later, Darcy buzzed me on the intercom. "Detective Keating is on line one."

And I'd thought the morning couldn't get more depressing. Silly me.

I picked up the phone. "Skerritt here."

"Good morning to you, too." Keating's voice was as sexy as his appearance. Combine that with his arrogant personality, and he was downright irritating.

"What do you want?"

"Got up on the wrong side of the bed, did you?"

I was being rude, but my ill manners were rolling off his ego like rain off a newly waxed car. "Yes. So?"

"So I have an ID on your John Doe."

Between dealing with Trish and trying to reconcile Kimberly's fears, I'd forgotten about J.D. and the Lassiter sisters.

I reached for a pencil. "Okay."

"Not so fast," he said. "We have a deal, remember?"

Memory clicked. "Yeah, I remember. I'll meet you for lunch."

"Lunch wasn't our agreement. I'll pick you up at seven for dinner at Sophia's."

"I'll meet you at Sophia's," I corrected. I had the distinct impression that riding in the same car with Keating would turn him into an octopus with more appendages than I could handle. "Remember, we're two professionals having dinner to share information, so don't get any wise ideas."

He laughed as if I'd cracked a joke. "See you at seven, Maggie."

A FEW HOURS LATER, I'd decided that tonight's dinner with Keating was going to be a treat compared to my morning from hell.

When I had picked Trish up at the house after Keating's call, she'd looked none the worse for wear after the previous evening's overindulgence, especially once sunglasses covered her bloodshot eyes.

She fastened her seat belt as if impaling an enemy. "This is a waste of time."

"You're going back to Seattle?" I couldn't keep the hopefulness from my voice.

"No, but I know I won't see anything I like better than where I am now."

"Where you are now is *my* house."

"I'm sure Bill will buy out your half."

She was living in a dreamworld, but her real world had turned so ugly, maybe dreams were all she could face.

"I've picked out several great properties in good neighborhoods and arranged for the leasing agents to meet us there."

She leaned against the headrest and sighed. "At least I'll get some fresh air."

Three hours later, I wanted to cut off her air supply entirely. First, I'd driven her to the most elegant property, a one-bedroom condo on the approach to the causeway to Pelican Beach. The complex was built over a ground floor parking garage.

We climbed to the second floor, where the condo's sliders gave magnificent vistas of the bay, Pelican Beach and Caladesi and Honeymoon Islands, all framed by palms. The newly renovated space was small but packed with amenities: a washer/dryer, large walk-in shower, updated kitchen and a balcony that caught the onshore breezes and tropical sunsets.

Even though Bill had agreed to spring for the added cost of the upscale digs, Trish turned up her nose and shook her head. "Too many stairs."

Undeterred, I drove her to Countryside, not far from the mall. The attractive town house, nestled among trees and backing onto a conservation area, was quiet and luxurious and only minutes from serious shopping, one of Trish's passions.

"Not enough windows," she complained of the unit sandwiched between two others.

"But you have skylights," I said.

"Too claustrophobic." She walked out the front door and headed for the car. I thanked the agent and followed her.

I'd saved the best for last, a house for rent in Osprey Country Club Estates. Built in the fifties, the postmodern residence, beautifully restored and landscaped, was small but a perfect fit for one person.

Trish wandered through the rooms with copious windows and large expanses of glass in the gables of the vaulted ceilings.

"You'll have plenty of light here," I said. "Lots of windows, sliding glass doors."

"That's the problem," Trish said.

I shoved my hands in the pockets of my skirt to keep from strangling her. "Why are windows a problem?"

"With all this glass, anyone could break in, in a heartbeat. I'd be living alone, after all." She shook her head. "No, it would be too scary."

Scary was what was going to happen to her if she didn't move out of Bill's and my house. Soon.

Temporarily admitting defeat, I dropped her back at our place and left her mixing rum and Coke for a liquid lunch a little after noon.

Messy as it was, I might have to resort to dynamite to dislodge her after all.

CHAPTER 16

Later that afternoon, I met Bill at his boat and explained the failure of my mission.

"You'll just have to ask her to leave." We were sitting on the rear deck, enjoying the refreshing, salty breeze. "Trish has deluded herself into believing you two are going to take up where you left off all those years ago."

Bill frowned. "She's in a fragile state. I don't want to push her over the edge."

I was ready to push her off a cliff, which, lucky for Trish, wasn't available, considering Florida's flat terrain.

"Letting her stay alone, drinking all day, isn't helping her situation," I said.

"Wouldn't she do the same thing in her own apartment?"

"If she gets a job and recognizes that she can't continue to depend on you, maybe she'll pull herself together."

"Or go off the deep end entirely." Bill shook his head. "But you're right. She can't remain at our place. I'll call the leasing agent tomorrow and put a deposit on the condo on the causeway. And I'll rent her a car until I can find her a used one."

"No, until *she* can find one for herself," I said firmly. "As long as you're acting like a knight in shining armor, she's going to play damsel in distress. She has to take charge of her own life, or she'll come running to you for everything."

Bill reached across and grasped my hand. "It's strange how clear hindsight can be. Looking back on my marriage to Trish, I can see now how she relied on me for everything. I made all the decisions, handled the finances, disciplined Melanie. No wonder Trish was terrified something would happen to me. She wouldn't have known what to do without me."

"Then why did she strike out on her own?"

"Maybe she was facing her worst fears," he said.

"But she didn't. She married Harvey instead."

Bill nodded. "And my guess is that Harvey finally got tired of her dependency. At first, her clinging was probably flattering, but a marriage is a partnership. If her marriage to Harvey was like hers to me, Trish collected the benefits without any responsibility."

A flutter of my previous hesitancy about marrying swept over me. "Do I lean on you too much? I know I let you do all the cooking."

Bill laughed. "You, Margaret, are the most self-sufficient woman I know. And cooking for you is a joy, not a chore."

His praise reassured me. "Do you think we should approach Trish with a united front?" I said. "Both of us could help her pack and move."

"Good idea. That way she'll have no doubt where my loyalties and affection lie."

"As long as she's sober enough to think straight," I said.

"One can only hope."

"So," I said, feeling wifely, "how was your day?"

Bill shrugged. "I talked to several of Tonya McClain's friends and neighbors. She'd discussed her previous employment by Wynona Wisdom with two of her friends. Tonya had obvious issues with Kimberly."

"That's what Kimberly said. Tonya didn't agree with the advice Kimberly gave."

Bill reached down to Roger, who lay on the deck at his feet, and scratched behind the dog's ears. "Then Kimberly must not have known."

"Known what?"

"That Tonya had a thing for her."

"A thing?" I grinned, knowing what he meant but wanting him to say it.

"Tonya was in love with Kimberly."

I did a few mental calculations. "If I have the timeline right, that would have been about the time Kimberly went gaga over Simon Anderson."

Bill nodded.

"But," I added, "loving someone who doesn't love you back doesn't necessarily make you a killer. If so, we might as well arrest Trish right now."

"What if Tonya's unrequited love ate at her? Maybe, despite her insistence that she didn't know Kimberly had moved here, Tonya followed her to Tampa Bay and decided if she couldn't have Kimberly, nobody would."

"That's a stretch, but not out of the question."

"It's the only theory that fits our only suspect." His gaze followed three pelicans skimming in chevron formation across the sunlit water. "Otherwise, we're back to the random-sniper theory."

I nodded. "And a random killer leaves the door wide open for every suspect from nutcases to gang initiates."

"Which means Kimberly could spend the rest of her life wondering whether she is a target."

"Speaking of our client, can you stay with her this evening?"

He raised his eyebrows. "Sure. Where will you be?"

"On a not-so-hot date."

"Date? What part of *engaged* don't you understand?" he teased.

"The same part you forgot in bringing your ex-wife into our soon-to-be home."

"Touché. You don't take crap off anyone, do you?"

"Let's leave my mother out of this."

I explained how Keating had agreed to run J.D.'s prints and how he'd coerced me into having dinner with him before giving me what he'd discovered.

"Just do me one favor," Bill said.

"What's that?"

"Order the most expensive item on the menu."

I leaned over and kissed his very attractive mouth. "I'll bring you a go-box."

I HADN'T BEEN TO SOPHIA'S since June, when Bill and I, assisted by Adler, Porter and Mackley, had provided security for a reception following the wedding of a couple from two feuding families. The event had turned into a catastrophe, but we'd averted major damage to the restaurant's banquet room by putting our emergency plan into action and separating the combatants before furniture was broken or blood spilled.

I hoped I wasn't going to need an emergency plan tonight. Waiting in the lobby, Keating was drawing interesting stares from other women. In his well-cut suit and tie, he was appealing eye candy to those unaware of his self-centered personality.

Nobody noticed me. Unlike my sister Caroline, who lived and died by the latest issue of *Vogue*, I was no fashion hound. My navy linen dress, worn tonight without its matching jacket due to the heat, was ages old and the dowdiest thing I owned. I'd bought it while working with the Pelican Bay PD to wear for court appearances and had hoped its ho-hum style would send Keating a message. But the guy's clue radar was apparently shut down for repair.

He gave a low whistle when he saw me. "Maggie, you look fabulous."

"Thanks." I nodded toward the large manila envelope in his hand. "Is that what you found on J.D.?"

My urge was to snatch it and run.

He nodded. "But what's your hurry? We have all night."

I shuddered at the anticipation in his voice. "You may have all night. I have a client waiting for me."

He offered me his arm. "Then we shouldn't waste any time."

Stiffening my back and my resolve to get dinner over with as soon as possible, I rested my hand lightly on his sleeve. We followed the maître d' down broad marble stairs into the dining room.

Sophia's had been built in the style of a Venetian palazzo, and its soaring ceiling, encircling balcony and rococo ornamentation made the restaurant a visual as well as a culinary delight. The room's linen-draped tables were crowded with diners, and soft music and the muted clink of silverware and crystal filled the air.

The maître d' led us to a secluded alcove beside an arched window that overlooked the sound. Beside the table, champagne chilled in a silver bucket. A single red rose lay beside my place setting.

It looked as if Keating had received an A in Seduction 101. Make that a B+, points lost for the missing gypsy violinist.

The maître d' pulled out my chair, seated me and flicked a heavy linen napkin onto my lap. He handed us each a leather-bound menu. Then the waiter, hovering nearby, stepped forward to open the champagne.

"Just water for me," I said.

Keating's face fell. "But, Maggie, this is a celebration."

"This is business. And alcohol reacts with my medication." I'd mixed Benadryl with a vodka tonic once and, to my mother's horror, had fallen asleep at the table at the Pelican Bay Yacht Club. With Keating, I needed my wits about me.

"Medication?" he said. "You're not ill?"

My hives were none of his business, but I couldn't resist the opportunity to yank his chain. "The doctor says I'm no threat to anyone as long as I take my pills."

The waiter filled my water glass and Keating's champagne flute.

"I'm ready to order," I said. "I'll have the surf and turf and a Greek salad."

Keating's pained expression as he ordered his steak rare told me events were moving too fast for him.

The waiter left, and Keating raised his glass and fixed me with a heated stare. "To us."

I lifted my water goblet. "To us finding J.D.'s family."

I shifted my gaze to the manila envelope by his plate. "I can read that while we wait for our food."

As if afraid I'd make a lunge for it, he placed his hand on the envelope. "Why don't we talk instead?"

"About what?"

"About you." He smiled, slow and sexy, and his voice was a caress. "I want to know everything about you."

I bit back a sharp reply. Keating, after all, was doing me a favor by running J.D.'s prints and buying dinner. I tried to be nice. "There's nothing to know. I was a cop, now I'm a P.I. and about to be married to a man I've loved for years."

"And nothing will change your mind?"

I shook my head. "So you might as well give up."

"It's against my nature."

"Why aren't you married?"

He shrugged.

A guy as handsome as Keating was probably used to women who fell all over him. Maybe only the ones who didn't intrigued him. "Seems to me you're a man who likes the chase but loses interest after he's made the catch."

His smile faded. Apparently, I'd hit too close to home.

"You a shrink as well as a P.I.?" he asked.

I shook my head and smiled to soften my words. "But in our business, we have to know how to read people."

"I'm not saying you're right."

"I've been wrong before." But this time I didn't

think so. I was pretty sure I had Keating pegged. When he quickly abandoned his seduction and got down to business, I was certain.

"Your John Doe's ex-military." He handed me the envelope. "And I did some more snooping for you. It's all in there."

I opened the flap and pulled out two sheets of paper. The top sheet contained a photo of a much younger J.D. in a Marine uniform. I scanned the info.

"Served in Vietnam," I said. "Decorated for valor."

"His name is Thomas Burke."

"Any priors?"

Keating shook his head. "According to National Crime Information Center, his record is clean. I ran his name through the Department of Motor Vehicles in New York, his home state. The results are there."

I flipped the page and discovered another more recent photo on a copy of a New York driver's license. J.D. was wearing a clerical collar. The Lassiter sisters' tenant was a priest.

CHAPTER 17

The next morning Darcy brought hot drinks and glazed doughnuts from the bookstore coffee bar downstairs and placed them on my desk. Taking her cup of green tea and a pastry, she sat across from me. At her feet, Roger watched for errant crumbs.

"You rid of that woman yet?" she asked.

"Which one?"

"The one living in your house."

"Which house?"

She shook her head. "Girl, your life is a mess. A freaked-out advice slinger and a drunken ex-wife, both camping out on your various doorsteps."

I reached for my coffee. "Good reason to leave town this weekend. Bill and I are going on a cruise."

"'Bout time you two spent some quality time together. I hear you had dinner last night with Deputy Do-Right."

"You heard? How?"

"I have my sources."

I glanced at my desktop and saw "Keating, 7:00 p.m., Sophia's" penciled on my day planner. Darcy's source was reading my calendar. "You bucking for a promotion from administrative assistant to investigator?"

"I'm just wondering what the hell is going on. Bill with his ex-wife, you going out with Keating. When are things getting back to normal around here?"

"Depends on what you call normal."

"You know what I mean," she said in a huff. "You and Bill against the world, like it's always been."

"Then things are back to normal," I said.

"Uh-uh." Darcy gave me a disgusted look. "Not as long as that she-devil is staking a claim on your house and your man and you're flirting with the enemy."

She was going to keep at me until I explained. Knowing her nosiness grew out of concern, I relented. "Bill and I are telling Trish this afternoon that we're putting her on a plane to her daughter's in Seattle. And Keating insisted I have dinner with him to give me the identity of the Lassiter sisters' John Doe."

Darcy cocked an eyebrow. "He coulda told you over the phone."

"Once he exhausted his God's-gift-to-women routine without effect, dinner wasn't so bad. His overblown ego covers a lot of insecurity."

"So what now?"

"Now I need you to find me the phone number of diocese headquarters in Rochester, N.Y. Apparently, they're missing a priest."

Darcy wrinkled her brow. "Your John Doe's a priest, and you're working on the murder of a nun? Isn't that a coincidence?"

"Maybe."

"Or maybe J.D. was an assassin sent by Opus Dei to knock off the sister."

I rolled my eyes. "You've been reading too many Dan Brown books. More likely God's trying to tell me something."

Darcy gave Roger her last crumb of doughnut and pushed to her feet. "Just don't make Him come down here."

TWO HOURS LATER, I pulled into the Lassiter driveway. No one answered when I knocked at the front door, but I could hear sounds of tapping coming from the backyard. I walked around the house through the carport and spotted J.D., removing the broken pane from the shed window.

His T-shirt, damp with sweat, stuck to his skin, and his legs and arms, exposed by cutoffs and short sleeves, were tanned. He greeted me with a warm smile.

"You're a persistent woman, Maggie Skerritt. But I'm not giving you my fingerprints."

"Persistence pays off, Father Tom."

He set aside the broken shards of glass and stared. "Father Tom?"

"I've found out who you are."

Looking frightened, he shook his head. "Don't tell me."

"I think you want to know. You've got a job to do."

With a sigh, he motioned toward the back porch. "It's cooler in the shade."

I followed him onto the porch and took a seat on an old metal glider, rusty and in need of paint. He sat across from me in an aluminum lawn chair with nylon webbing. He had the look of a man facing sentencing. Or execution.

"Your dreams of blood and death," I said, "are flashbacks from Vietnam. You were a Marine lieutenant." I handed him the first page from Keating's envelope. "You were awarded the Purple Heart and Silver Star."

He took the page, read through it and handed it back to me. "That man is a stranger. Nothing there seems familiar."

"I spoke with your bishop this morning. He knows your story. When you returned from the war, your spirit was broken. You were disillusioned. In a search for meaning, you entered seminary and became a priest. You've been a fine priest ever since."

"That's why you called me Father Tom." He shook his head. "Why can't I remember?"

"That's what we want to find out. The bishop faxed me copies of your medical insurance. You need to see a neurologist."

He flashed a thin smile. "Have my head examined?"

I nodded.

"I must have fallen on the trail and hit my head. That's why I can't remember."

"It's more complicated than that," I said. "After speaking with the bishop, I talked with the manager of the hotel on Pelican Beach where you were staying on vacation in July. He remembers you. The night before you vacated your room, you won $10,000 on a casino cruise. You apparently have a flair for poker."

Recognition flickered in his eyes. "I played poker with the guys in Nam. I'm beginning to remember."

"According to the manager, the next day you rented a bike for a ride on the trail. He never saw you again."

"Did they call the police when I didn't return for the things in my room?"

"But you did return."

He raised his gray eyebrows in surprise. "I don't remember."

"Because it wasn't you. From what I've been able to piece together, someone who knew you'd won big on the cruise followed you on the trail. You were attacked, knocked out and robbed."

"But surely I wouldn't have carried all that money on me."

"You didn't. The manager said you'd locked it in the hotel safe before you left to go biking."

"Then the money's still there?"

I shook my head. "Whoever robbed you stole your ID and room key. He must have gone back to the hotel, taken your clothes and other belongings and requested the money from the safe."

"But if the manager knew me, he wouldn't have given the money to a stranger."

"The assistant manager didn't know you. When your assailant, dressed in your clerical collar and carrying your room key, checked out, she gave him the money he requested."

"So no one at the hotel knew I was missing?"

"Not until the Rochester police contacted them a week later. The bishop called them after talking to the airlines. Someone using your identification papers boarded in Tampa for the flight to Rochester. The bishop thought you'd returned to the city and then disappeared. That's why no one was looking for you down here. The thief must have used your plane ticket to get out of town. For all we know, he could be anywhere now, even Canada."

"And the bishop…" J.D. hesitated. "Did he really say I was a good priest?"

"The best. That's why he's anxious to have you back. Your entire parish has missed you. And your family."

"Family?"

"You have a twin sister, Emily."

"Emily." His voice caressed the name and another flicker of remembrance lit his eyes.

"And you have children and grandchildren," I said.

His eyes widened with shock. "But I'm a priest."

"You married while you were in college and had two children. Your wife divorced you while you were in Vietnam. But you've kept in touch with your children and their families. They're anxious to see you."

Tears misted his eyes. "And I thought I was all alone."

"Far from it." I pulled a slip of paper from my pocket. "Here's the name and number of a neurologist at Pelican Bay Hospital. He treated my mother last spring. Tell his office I referred you and make an appointment, okay?"

"But what about home?"

"If Dr. Katz says you're in shape to fly, we'll put you on the next plane to Rochester."

He sat back in his chair and looked stunned. "I don't know what to say. Except thank you."

I'd almost forgotten. I dug into my other pocket. "Here's the name and address of the hotel in town where the bishop has arranged for you to stay for now. He's overnighting funds and your ticket home."

"That takes care of everything," J.D. said, then frowned. "Except the Lassiter sisters. Who will take care of them?"

"The Moore family next door," I said, "and I'll check on Violet and Bessie often."

He nodded, obviously comfortable with my assessment. "You're a good woman, Maggie. And not bad as a detective, either."

CHAPTER 18

On his boat, Bill made sandwiches for lunch, and I told him the saga of Father Tom.

"Too bad the trail's gone cold on his assailant," Bill said. "I'd love to see that guy thrown behind bars."

I sat at the booth in the galley, and Bill handed me a plate with a king-size sandwich, my favorite, sliced turkey with romaine.

"Not much chance of catching him now," I said. "The surveillance tapes at the hotel have been erased, the room's been cleaned a hundred times and Father Tom had only cash, no credit cards to trace."

"So…" Bill sat across from me and passed a bag of potato chips. "That's one mystery solved. Now if we can find Sister Mary Theresa's killer, we'll be batting a thousand."

I swallowed a bite of turkey on whole wheat. "He, or she, is as far off the radar as Father Tom's assailant. No more similar shootings have been reported anywhere in the country. And, according to security at the gate at Kimberly's condo, no one's been asking for her and no sign of anyone hanging around as if to get a look."

Bill munched chips, his expression thoughtful. "Could be the shooter hasn't worked up the nerve to hit again. Or is simply waiting for another target of opportunity."

"You don't think someone's specifically after Kim?"

"Who would it be? The ex-fiancé is out of the country."

"What about Tonya McClain?"

He shook his head. "I can't see it. She was completely open about working for Kim when I interviewed her."

"Not exactly. She didn't bother to mention her unrequited love."

"Maybe she's over it," he said. "It's been a few years, after all."

I wasn't so easily convinced. "Okay, maybe it's not Tonya. But that fact doesn't rule out potentially hundreds of wacko readers whom Wynona Wisdom has ticked off over the years. We've only scratched the surface on those nutcases."

"So how long does the poor girl stay in hiding?" he asked. "That's no way to live."

I reached across the table with my napkin and

removed a smear of mayonnaise from Bill's chin. "I need more time. I can't get over the feeling that I'm missing something. Maybe with other distractions out of the way, I'll be able to figure out what it is."

Bill smiled, kick-starting my pulse rate. "Distractions? Like Trish? Or maybe Keating?"

"Keating?" I grimaced. I'd had my fill of the egotistical sheriff's detective. "I was thinking of Father Tom but, now that you mention your ex, we need a plan to convince her to get out of our house."

"Evictions are always difficult," he said with a scowl. "We had to oversee our share of them in the good old days as patrol officers, didn't we?"

I nodded, remembering. "Kicking out deadbeats was satisfying. It was the families down on their luck who broke my heart."

"You could definitely say Trish is down on her luck," he said with compassion.

I could see his sympathy for his ex-wife building and feared he might lose his resolve to send her away. "Sometimes we create our own luck. Trish has to take control of her life and stop being dependent on others."

"A hard lesson to learn at any stage of life, but harder still at sixty."

I wasn't totally heartless. I felt sorry for Trish and her situation, but I also knew that pity wasn't the answer to her problem. Maybe by finally hitting bottom, she'd realize she needed major changes in her life. If not, nothing Bill nor I could do would help. "You made her plane reservations?"

"She leaves Tampa this evening at seven. I couldn't get a through flight. She'll have to change planes in Chicago."

"And Melanie's expecting her?"

He made a face. "I spent an hour on the phone with her this morning. I'm ashamed how little empathy my daughter has for her own mother. But I did convince Melanie to meet the plane. I left it up to her whether she wants to check Trish into rehab. My guess is she'll try, if for no other reason than to relieve herself of the responsibility."

I eyed Bill carefully. "You agreed to cover the costs, didn't you?"

His blue eyes widened in surprise. "How did you know?"

"One, because Trish can't afford it. Two, because Melanie is too selfish to volunteer and three, because I know you."

"You don't think I should?"

I rose from my side of the booth and slid onto the cushion next to him. "I think you're the best person I've ever known. And I'm sure I don't deserve you."

He slid his arms around me. "I believed my world had fallen apart all those years ago when Trish left me. Now, the more I'm around her, the more I thank my lucky stars that I have you."

His kiss tasted of salt and mayonnaise, and I was enjoying every minute of it until the distinctive ring of his cell phone interrupted our pleasure.

"Let it go," I whispered against his lips.

He hesitated. "It might be important."

I sighed and broke away. "One day when you're not looking, I'm going to throw that pesky thing overboard."

He pulled the phone from the carrier on his belt and checked the caller ID. "It's coming from the phone at our house."

"Trish. I should have known. She's been insinuating herself into our lives for too long now."

He flipped the phone open, and I could hear Trish screaming from where I sat.

"He's going to kill me!" Clear and unslurred, her words were filled with spine-tingling panic that would have been hard to fake.

"Take a deep breath," Bill spoke in his calm, reassuring voice, "and tell me what's happening."

"He broke into the house," Trish managed to enunciate between sobs, "and threatened me with a knife.

I'm locked in the bathroom now, but that lock won't hold him off long. He's beating on the door."

I jumped to my feet and reached for my purse and car keys.

"Have you called the police?" Bill asked as he slid out of the booth after me.

"No," Trish screamed, so loud I could still hear every word. "I thought you were closer, on your boat."

"I'm on the way."

By now, Bill and I were both on the dock, running toward my Volvo.

"Hang up," Bill told her. "Call 9-1-1 and stay on the line with them until we get there."

"Hurry, he's trying to break down the door!"

"Call 9-1-1," Bill ordered her again and snapped his phone shut.

I reached the car, slid into the driver's seat and Bill climbed in on the passenger side. Even at high speed, our house was a good three minutes away. I backed out of the parking space, stomped the gas and swerved around an approaching pickup pulling a boat trailer.

Three minutes to reach Trish. A lot could happen in three minutes.

And none of it good.

CHAPTER 19

I broke every traffic law on the books during the mile drive inland, speeding, running stop signs and passing on a double yellow line. I longed for the portable flashing light and siren from my days as a Pelican Bay detective, but made up for their absence by turning on my hazard lights and laying on the horn.

A green-and-white sheriff's cruiser was pulling to the curb in front of our house when Bill and I arrived. We jumped from the car and ran toward the deputy. In the distance, the siren from the officer's backup sounded.

"You folks stay back," the deputy ordered.

Bill showed his ID. "This is our house. We're both former cops. We're armed and we can help."

"Malcolm," the deputy said with a flicker of recognition. "I've heard of you."

He took only an instant to make a decision. Judging from the faint wail of the siren, his backup was still blocks away. "I'll take the rear door. You go in the front."

Bill shoved his ID in his pocket, dug out his keys and

raced up the curving walkway toward the front door. Gun drawn, I followed. Bill unlocked the door, removed his weapon from the holster at the back of his waist and swung the door open. He stepped quickly inside, checked the room, yelled, "Clear," and I joined him.

Together we swept the house, searching for the intruder. We ended in the master bedroom, where the bathroom door was closed but its surface showed signs of abuse.

"Trish," Bill called, "you okay?"

For a few seconds, his voice echoed in the room, followed by a long moment of silence. I tried not to picture what we might find on the other side of the door.

Then the lock clicked and the bathroom door swung inward. We both tensed, guns ready. Trish stood in the bathroom, her face pale, her body trembling.

"Is he gone?" she asked.

"You're safe," Bill said in the same tone he might have used with a spooked animal. "The house is clear. We've checked every room. He must have run when he heard the siren."

"Thank God," Trish said with a nod and crumpled to the floor in a heap.

Bill holstered his gun, rushed to her and lifted her from the cold tiles. I followed as he carried her to the sofa in the living room, where we met the deputy, who'd come in the back way.

"She okay?" he asked.

I checked Trish for signs of injuries and found none. Her breathing and pulse were steady, and her eyelids flickered as consciousness returned.

"Just scared witless," I said. "Did you catch the intruder?"

The deputy shook his head. "He left a trail of broken branches where he took off through the backyard. Two other units are chasing him, and I've called in the K-9 and helicopter."

With a low moan, Trish raised herself on her elbows.

"Can you give me a description?" the deputy asked her.

"A tall guy," she murmured. "He was carrying a big knife."

"Kitchen knife?" I asked.

Trish shook her head. "Looked like a hunting knife. He wore a ski mask, dark shirt, dark pants. And gloves."

"No prints, then," I commented.

"How'd he get in?" Bill asked.

The deputy nodded toward the kitchen. "Cut the glass in the back door, reached in and flipped the lock."

Trish was sitting up now with her arms wrapped around her. She was shivering and her teeth chattered, so I took an afghan from Bill's chair and draped it across her shoulders. As annoying as her presence had been, she hadn't deserved being traumatized.

Bill crossed the room to a low mission-style cabinet beside the fireplace, opened its doors and removed a bottle of brandy and a cut crystal glass. He poured a generous shot of the amber liquid and handed it to Trish. "Drink this."

Trish didn't need coaxing. She belted the drink down in one swallow and held out the glass for more. Bill took the empty glass but didn't return to the cabinet.

"Nothing else in the house appears disturbed," he told the deputy. "I don't think robbery was a motive."

The deputy, Ryker, according to the name badge on his uniform, nodded. "Could have been a sex offender."

Trish squealed in alarm. "A rapist?"

"He didn't hurt you, did he, ma'am?" Ryker asked.

"He never laid a finger on me. I was just sitting here watching TV and looked up and there he was. Scared me to death. Although from the way he flinched when he saw me, I think I surprised him, too. I didn't hang around to ask why. I took off toward the back of the house and locked myself in the bathroom."

"He didn't say anything?" I asked.

Trish thought for a minute, then nodded. "But it didn't make any sense."

"What did he say?" Bill prompted.

Trish shook her head. "Something like 'you're not Kimberly.'"

Bill and I exchanged a long look. My gut had apparently been right. Someone really was out to get Kimberly Ross, aka Wynona Wisdom.

"When I was locked in the bathroom," Trish continued, "he kept beating on the door and yelling 'where is she?'"

"Are you sure it was a male?" I asked.

The brandy had apparently had a relaxing effect. Trish, who'd ceased shivering, snorted. "You ever hear of a female rapist?"

The deputy was eyeing me with skepticism, but I pressed ahead. "Could the person who broke in have been a tall, muscular female? Did the voice give any clues?"

Trish shrugged. "The voice was deep. Angry."

"What about build?" Bill asked. "Any visible curves?"

"You think you have a suspect?" the deputy asked.

Not wanting to implicate Tonya McClain without proof, I shook my head. "Old habits die hard. As former detectives, we're just covering all the bases."

"The guy's clothes were baggy," Trish said. "I couldn't tell anything about his physique, except that he was tall. Not that I was checking," she added with a frown. "I was too busy getting away." She looked at Bill. "I need another drink."

He shook his head. "My guess is that you haven't eaten, have you?"

"I had coffee for breakfast," she said.

The crime scene unit had arrived and were processing the kitchen, where, unless they were lucky, I doubted they'd find anything. Gloves meant no prints, ski mask meant no loose hairs and the dry bricks of the courtyard meant no footprints.

"As soon as CSU is finished in the kitchen," Bill said to Trish, "I'll fix you something to eat."

She shook her head. "I don't want to eat. I want to go home."

"Home?" I didn't have the heart to remind her that she no longer had a home.

"I don't feel safe here," Trish said. "Especially by myself."

The deputy went into the kitchen to talk to the

crime techs. I sat in a chair across from Trish, but Bill remained standing, one elbow propped on the mantel.

"You won't have to stay alone any longer," he said.

Hope flared in Trish's green eyes. "You're moving in?"

Bill shook his head. "You're flying out this evening for Seattle. Melanie will meet you at the airport."

"But—"

Bill cut her off. "It was wrong for me to let you stay here. In our business, Maggie and I run into all kinds of dangerous people who wish to harm us or our clients. That's what happened today. Someone was looking for one of our clients and thought she might be staying here."

Trish's mouth gaped in horror. "You mean things like this happen often?"

"Not often," I said, "but they're always a possibility."

"And I can't in good conscience keep you in that kind of situation," Bill added. "You'll be safe in Seattle with Melanie. She's agreed to help you."

"Help me?"

"Find a house, a job. And you'll be near the grandchildren."

At the mention of her grandkids, Trish's face softened, and I knew at that moment that getting her on the flight would be no problem.

I stood and motioned for Bill to join me. We stepped outside onto the front porch.

"I'm going to my condo to check on Kim. You can fill the deputies in on our case, if you like, but as soon as I know Kim's okay, I'm calling Adler."

Bill nodded. "We'll need a new safe house for her, one not connected to either of us."

"Which raises the question, how did the intruder know about this address?"

"Good point," Bill said. "My guess is that since we're no longer cops, the recent purchase of this house went into the public records when we bought this place. If someone was looking for us, this address is under our names on the tax rolls."

"Call Darcy," I said. "The intruder may try the office. Tell her to close up and go to her mother's until we give an all clear."

"I'm on it."

"What about your car?" I asked.

"I'll ask one of the deputies to drop me off at the marina to pick it up."

I nodded. "Be careful."

"You, too. Call me when you get home."

I gave him a quick kiss and hurried to my car. I'd purchased my condo while I was a cop, so it wasn't listed on the public records, but a few casual questions around town could have pointed Kim's stalker in the right direction.

I broke a few more traffic laws driving home.

CHAPTER 20

All appeared normal when I reached my condo, but I wasn't taking any chances. I drew my gun before unlocking the front door and eased inside with caution.

A heavy blow to my calves nearly brought me down.

"Roger!" I shouted. "You scared me to death!"

Unrepentant, Roger didn't miss a beat in his canine happy dance, making me feel mean for yelling at him. A quick survey of the downstairs revealed no signs of intrusion.

"Maggie," Kim called from the upstairs spare room, "is that you?"

"Hey, Kim," I shouted up the stairwell. "Don't let me disturb you if you're working."

"I have one more letter to answer, then I'll be down."

I relaxed for the first time since leaving Bill at the other house. All was apparently safe and quiet on the home front. "No hurry. I have some calls to make."

I went into the living room, grabbed the handset

and dialed Bill's cell phone to let him know I'd arrived and that everything was okay. Then I called Adler.

"I have some activity on your sniper case," I said when he answered.

"Not another murder, I hope."

"Not yet." I gave him the details on the break-in at our place and the intruder who had accosted Trish. "Sheriff's deputies have a manhunt ongoing."

"You think they'll find him?"

"They're using helicopter and K-9 units, but my guess is, if the intruder had any sense, he left a car nearby and is now long gone."

"Thanks for the heads up," Adler said. "First thing I'll do is call CENTCOM and see if Tonya McClain is working today."

"I'll be moving Kim to another location ASAP," I said. "Apparently, she was the target of our intruder, and he or she is hot on Kim's trail."

"Where will Kim go?" Adler asked.

"I'll check with Abe. He may be able to put her up at his house, at least until we can find somewhere else. It can't be any place connected to me or anyone at Pelican Bay Investigations. Abe's not officially on the payroll, so his place should be safe."

"How did the shooter know where to look for her?" Adler said.

"Good question. And the answer will tell us a lot we don't know now. Let me know what you find out about McClain."

"Will do."

I ended the call with Adler to find Kim standing behind me, obviously shaken, her eyes round with fear, her face pale.

"You heard?" I asked.

She nodded. "I was beginning to think maybe you were right, that Sister Mary Theresa's death was a random sniping. But the intruder at the other house asked specifically for me, didn't he?"

"He asked where Kimberly was," I said, "no last name. But we'd be foolish not to assume he meant you, under the circumstances."

"You think 'he' might have been Tonya?"

"Detective Adler's checking out that angle."

"What do I do now?" She had the frantic, desperate look of a cornered animal and latent hysteria edged her voice.

I decided a no-nonsense approach was best. "We're moving you to a safer place, so you'd better start packing."

Kim nodded and turned to leave.

"Wait," I said. "I need some answers first."

She turned back and sank into a wicker rocker as

if the muscles in her legs had failed. "What do you want to know?"

"Who have you talked to at your office since you moved in here?"

She thought for a second. "Just Cindy and Gerry."

"And you didn't tell them where you are?"

Kim shook her head. "You said it was important that I didn't, that everything go through Pelican Bay Investigations. I made all the calls on my cell phone, so your phone number wouldn't show up on caller ID."

"Call your office now," I said, "and see who's there."

She removed her cell phone from the pocket of her denim shorts and punched a few numbers. "Hey, it's me," she said when someone answered. "Who's working today?"

She listened to the voice on the other end of the line, then said, "You're sure nobody took off early?"

She listened again, then flipped the phone shut. "Everyone's still in Omaha, so you can rule out my employees."

"Even Steve…what's his name?"

"Steve Haggerty. He's still on vacation, so it couldn't have been him. He's in Alaska photographing grizzly bears. Denali National Park."

"You're sure?"

She nodded. "Cindy says he checks in with the office every day."

"Why would he do that?"

She squared her shoulders in a defensive posture. "He is my chief assistant, after all. He feels responsible for keeping the office running smoothly. And he's been concerned for my safety since Sister Mary Theresa was killed."

A question popped into my mind, one I kicked myself for not asking before. "What happens to the 'Ask Wynona Wisdom' column if you die?"

Kim smiled. "She'll keep on giving advice. I've arranged to transfer the rights to Steve. He did such a great job before when I was out sick, I think he'd keep the column going without a problem."

"If Steve owned the rights, he could make a lot of money, couldn't he?" I asked. "As much as you have?"

"Sure, but—" She shook her head. "What are you implying?"

"When I asked who stood to gain by your death, you told me the beneficiaries from your will. You didn't mention the rights to your column."

"I didn't think of it. That's a separate transaction that includes a key man insurance policy. Besides, it's irrelevant. Steve wouldn't hurt me. We're friends. We work great together, and he's well-compensated, too."

She sounded as if she was trying to convince herself as much as me.

"You have any hard proof Steve is actually in Alaska?" I said.

She shook her head. "Just the telephone reports of his adventures that he gives the office every day." Her expression brightened. "He e-mailed me some photos he took in the park."

My skepticism was one of my best detecting tools. "Was Steve in any of them?"

With a sigh and a frown, Kim shook her head. "If he's taking the pictures, he wouldn't be in them."

"But he could have taken the photos off the Internet?" I knew only enough about computers to be dangerous, but even I was familiar with the process called *cut and paste*.

"Why would he do that?" Kim insisted.

"To establish an alibi."

Her mouth hardened into a thin, tight line. "I don't believe it. Steve's been my friend for too long. He wouldn't hurt me."

"Not even for the money?"

"Not even—"

The starch went out of her posture, and she slumped like a rag doll. "Oh, no."

"What?"

"He asked to borrow a large amount of cash before he left on vacation."

"Did he say why he needed it?" I asked.

Kim squirmed and the wicker in her chair creaked. "I promised I'd keep his secret."

"Someone tried to kill you this afternoon," I reminded her. "If you'd been at the other house instead of here, you could be dead now. If Steve's need for money isn't related to your stalker, his secrets are safe with me."

Kim appeared to reconsider, then grimaced. "Poker debts."

"Steve owed money?"

She nodded.

"How much?"

"Twenty-five thousand dollars."

"And you loaned it to him?" I asked.

"Yes, so, you see, he had no reason to kill me. I gave him what he needed."

If twenty-five grand was *all* he needed. "But he still has to pay you back."

"I'll deduct it from his paycheck over the next few years," she said, "so it's not a problem."

"Why would someone who's up to his eyeballs in debt take a trip to Alaska?" I asked. "Airfare and accommodations aren't cheap."

Kim shrugged. "Maybe he was stressed out. Or maybe he wanted to get away from the guys he owed money to."

"But you loaned him the money to pay them back. Things aren't adding up for Mr. Haggerty."

Kim looked sick to her stomach, and I couldn't blame her. The possibility of having a trusted employee and friend out to kill you would make anyone sick.

"You'd better go upstairs and pack," I said. "We're moving you to a safer place as soon as you're ready."

She pushed to her feet as if the world's weight were on her shoulders. "Where?"

I grinned. "It's so secret, even I don't know where it is yet."

My lame attempt at humor failed to cheer her, and she headed upstairs to pack.

The phone rang and, expecting Adler, I picked up the handset. "What did you find out?"

A long, cold silence greeted me.

"Hello?" I said.

The person on the other end sighed heavily. "Margaret, I would hope that after almost fifty years, I could have instilled some proper sense of telephone etiquette in you."

"Hello, Mother. You still in New York?"

"I've been home for days, which you would know if you'd bothered to check on me."

My inner child winced with guilt, but I'd developed a tough outer shell over the years to protect myself from Mother's barbs. "I called when the storm was coming to make sure you had a safe place to evacuate." Which was more than she'd done for me. "Didn't Estelle tell you?"

"That was days ago." What Mother didn't want to talk about, she circumvented or ignored. "I'm calling about Sunday."

My gut clenched. "What about Sunday?"

"I've made reservations at the club for noon. I'll expect you and your Mr. Malcolm then."

I tried not to grind my teeth. "Mother, we're in the middle of a murder investigation—"

"You have to eat, Margaret, no matter what you're doing. I'll see you then."

Without giving me a chance to refuse, she hung up.

Only then did I remember the weekend cruise Bill and I had planned. I hastily scribbled a reminder to call her back and cancel once Kim was moved to a safer place, and slapped the sticky note on the refrigerator.

I dialed Abe Mackley's house. Within minutes, I'd arranged for us to drop Kim at his place on our way to the airport. He would take her from there to his fishing cabin on the Rainbow River near Dunellon.

I explained the plan to Kim when she carried her first load of belongings downstairs.

"Does he have a phone line for my fax at his river place?" she asked.

I nodded. "And good cell phone coverage. I checked. You should be able to keep in touch with your office without any trouble."

Kim rolled her eyes. "And the people who write to me think *they've* got problems."

She climbed the stairs for another load.

My phone rang again.

Learning from my recent mistake, I answered more decorously. "Hello."

"I called CENTCOM," Adler said.

"And?"

"We may have a suspect."

"Tonya's not there?"

"Nope," Adler said. "She called in sick today."

CHAPTER 21

"Did you call McClain's house, too?" I asked.

"Yep," Adler said. "No answer."

"I hate when that happens." I had pretty much ruled out McClain as a suspect, but the fact that she hadn't been at work when the break-in occurred raised serious red flags.

"Ralph and I are going to drive over to her place now," Adler said. "See if we can track her down."

"I guess that means the sheriff's search turned up nada."

"I talked to Detective Keating," Adler said. "The K-9 lost the scent on the street behind your house. Like you said, the intruder must have had a car."

"So if it was Tonya," I said, "she'd have had plenty of time to return home by now."

"Probably," Adler said, "but we have to interview her. She's the only lead we've got."

"Not anymore." I filled him in on Steve Haggerty and my suspicions.

"I'll contact the Omaha PD," he said. "Ask them to give us a hand in locating Haggerty."

"Keep me informed, okay?"

"Will do."

I heard the rattle of paper right before he hung up and knew he was either unwrapping a candy bar or opening a bag of chips. When a case got tough, I developed hives. Adler ate, even more than usual. It was a wonder that I had any skin left or that Adler didn't weigh 500 pounds.

BY THE TIME BILL arrived, Kim and I had her belongings packed and stacked just inside the front entrance. When I opened the door for Bill, I could see Trish, slumped in the passenger seat, head back, eyes closed.

"Did you give her a tranquilizer?" I asked him.

He straightened from greeting Roger with a pat. "Didn't have to. I thought she was packing in the guest room. I didn't realize until too late that she'd taken the brandy with her. She polished off the whole bottle."

"You may have to carry her onto the plane," I said.

"I'm sure she won't be the first passenger to board drunk," he said. "Lots of people drown their fear of flying in alcohol."

"With luck, she'll sleep it off before she reaches Seattle."

"I hope so," he said, "for Melanie's sake."

We kept Kim inside, out of sight, while Bill stowed her luggage in the back of his SUV next to Trish's. Kim remained remarkably calm. Either she had the greatest trust in Bill and me to keep her safe, or she was becoming hardened to life on the run. Or maybe between Sister Mary Theresa's murder and the near-miss hurricane, Kim was merely blissfully numb. While Bill kept a wary eye for anyone who might be lurking, I hurried her and Roger into the backseat.

With the car packed to the brim and me sitting in the rear with Kim and Roger, I flashed back to the summers of my childhood when Mother had stitched name labels in my clothing before packing it in a steamer trunk. Dad had then loaded it into the station wagon. Then my parents had driven me to camp in the North Carolina mountains.

"Do I have to go?" I'd cried.

Daddy had cast sympathetic glances in the rearview mirror, but Mother had been adamant.

"You're nothing but a recluse, Margaret," she'd scolded. "You stay in your room all day, reading. Such isolation is not healthy for a growing child. You need fresh air and the company of friends."

"But I don't know anybody at camp. My friends are here. And I don't stay all day in my room. Patty and I

play tennis, and Ruth Anne swims with me at the club."
At six years old, I was terrified at the prospect of being
left alone in an unfamiliar place among strangers.

"You should be more like Caroline," Mother had
said, apparently oblivious to my distress. "She has
dozens of friends."

"Is that why *she* doesn't have to go to camp?" I'd
asked.

"She's off on a cruise with the Hendersons,"
Mother had said. "With both our girls having fun,
your father and I will have some time to ourselves."

Me, having fun? I'd rather have had all my teeth
pulled.

"Don't you want to go, pumpkin?" Daddy had said
with a worried frown.

"Of course, she does," Mother had replied before I
could answer. "She's a lucky young lady to have such
a privilege. It's a very exclusive and expensive camp.
She'd have to be extremely ungrateful not to appreciate this opportunity."

I was ungrateful, I'd thought rebelliously, but I'd
felt ashamed for my father to know it, so I'd mumbled
something about looking forward to the trip.

I'd spent a miserable six weeks, sleeping in a cabin
that was no more than a wooden floor with screen
walls and a leaky roof, using an outdoor latrine,

weaving tacky pot holders and constructing substandard birdhouses from twigs and glue. I wasn't the only camper who'd cried myself to sleep at night, but I'd buried my face in my pillow so the others wouldn't hear. I'd lain awake for hours wondering what I'd done to deserve exile to the wilderness.

But the worst of the experience had been the counselor we nicknamed the Iron Mistress, a high school gym teacher hired by the camp to oversee our physical activities. She had run us up mountain trails so steep we had to use our hands as well as feet for climbing. She'd forced us to plunge into icy lakes for early morning swims and lifesaving classes. Then she'd made us perform calisthenics until our muscles had screamed in protest and our lungs had heaved, gasping for air.

We dreaded the end of each day's session. The Iron Mistress had erected bars eight feet off the ground in one of the picnic shelters. When we'd finished our exercises for the day, she'd had us leap from the picnic benches, grab hold of the bars and hang by our hands until she told us to drop or until gravity had prevailed. We had been supposed to build up to suspending ourselves for five minutes at a time before we finished camp. She had this crazy theory that people caught in house or hotel fires died because they couldn't hang on to a window ledge long enough for firemen to get a net under them. She'd been determined that if any of "her girls" were ever caught in such a situation, they would survive. We'd all sworn our arms grew inches from her torture and that if summer didn't end soon, our knuckles would drag the ground when we walked.

Still, the Iron Mistress's lessons had had a lasting impact on me. She'd prepared me well for the rigors of physical training at the police academy, an area where most women washed out from the physical and mental stress. And she'd insured that I never booked a hotel room above the second floor for the rest of my life.

Until I was seventeen, I'd been banished to camp every year. I'd never understood my mother's triumphant expression as she and Daddy drove away each time, not until earlier this year, when a longtime family friend had explained how jealous my mother had always been of my father's unconditional affection for me. Because of her insecurities, Mother had been convinced that he'd loved me more than her and had resented my existence.

As a six-year-old, I hadn't understood, and even well into adulthood, I'd puzzled over my mother's animosity until the recent revelations about my parents' marriage had solved the mystery. Now I accepted the fact that my mother had never really loved me. I hated the knowledge, but had learned to live with it.

"Margaret?"

I'd been so lost in memory, for a moment I mistook the male voice from the driver's seat as my late father's.

"Did you pack a bag for yourself?" Bill asked.

"No."

"You can't stay at your place," he said. "It's too dangerous."

"I'll pick up some clothes later," I said.

"I'm really sorry," Kim spoke beside me. "I didn't mean to place others in danger, too."

Hearing the dismay in her voice, Roger snuggled against her and placed his head on her lap.

"It's not your fault," I assured her. "You didn't ask to be stalked. Once you're in a safe spot, we'll lay a trap for your hunter and put an end to this madness."

Kim reached over and squeezed my hand, apparently satisfied by my reply, not knowing that I hadn't a clue yet how we'd manage to catch her pursuer, especially since we didn't know who the enemy was.

Bill's cell phone rang, and he answered. After listening a few minutes, he hung up. "That was Abe. He offered to have us leave Roger with him since Darcy's with her mother. You'll enjoy the river, won't you, boy?"

Roger, perpetually game for anything, wagged his tail and woofed his approval. We stopped at the first

Publix we spotted and bought dog food and dishes before dropping Kim and Roger off at Mackley's in Tampa. Abe placed Kim's luggage and Roger's supplies in his car, Roger trotted happily after Kim without a backward glance and the trio climbed into the car and headed north toward Dunellon.

Through all of this, Trish dozed in the front seat of the SUV, probably just as well after the scare she'd suffered earlier in the afternoon.

Once Kim was safely on her way, Bill and I drove Trish to the airport. Between the two of us and the help of a friendly skycap with a wheelchair, we saw Trish safely boarded onto her flight.

She disappeared down the Jetway, and Bill turned to me and grinned. "I feel as if I've been rescued from beneath a ten-ton rock slide. After dealing with Trish and her emotional ups and downs the past few days, catching a killer will seem like a picnic."

I couldn't have agreed more. Trish's unexpected visit, a blast from the past that I could have done without, had proved several things: I wanted to live the rest of my life with Bill, his love for me was un-shakable and he was a man I could trust with my heart. I was one lucky woman to have him. I wouldn't make Trish's mistakes when it came to marriage, although I'd probably come up with some originals of my own. And with a love like ours, Bill and I would survive them all.

Sharing Bill's buoyancy, I followed him to his car. We'd just left short-term parking when his cell phone rang again.

"Adler," Bill said with a glance at the caller ID.

We were approaching the toll gate, so he handed me the phone before pulling out his wallet to pay the parking fee.

I flipped open the cell and placed it to my ear. "What's up?"

"Ralph and I have spent the past few hours staking out Tonya McClain's condo. Her car's there, but there's no sign of her. She's not answering her door or her phone."

"CENTCOM said she called in sick. Did you try the hospitals?" I asked.

Bill paid the parking attendant, the barrier lifted and we drove out of the airport.

"Ralph called them all," Adler said. "Even her doctor, whose name CENTCOM gave us. No luck."

"We're on our way back across the causeway," I said. "Give us time to stop for takeout, and we'll meet you at Tonya's place. We'll take over the stakeout, and you can go home to a late supper."

Ever since Jessica's close call and the damage to their house during the recent storm, Sharon had been a bundle of nerves. Having her husband home for the evening would be good for her.

"You sure?" Adler asked.

I threw Bill a questioning glance and he nodded in agreement.

"No problem. See you soon."

CHAPTER 22

Bill and I took up surveillance in a parking lot across from Tonya's condo, a complex similar to most other condominiums in the area, multiple two-story buildings with covered carports out front and walkways on each floor that connected the units. They reminded me of mausoleums, and I often wondered why, when the owners died, the units weren't simply sealed and a personalized marker with R.I.P. affixed to the door.

The sun had set, but the temperature was in the high eighties and the humidity even higher, so we kept the SUV windows up and the motor running for the air-conditioning. Even if the weather had been cooler, we'd have needed the windows closed. The parking lot bordered wetlands, and salt marsh mosquitoes were swarming in clouds and throwing themselves against the windows as if aware blood and sustenance lay on the other side of the glass.

I thought of the idealized versions of Florida propagated by tourist bureaus and chambers of commerce throughout the state. Reading a colorful brochure or watching a television ad was conveniently deceptive, causing tourists and new residents to descend on the state in droves thicker than the flying insects outside my window. What the ads didn't reveal was the saunalike humidity, the bugs, the traffic and wall-to-wall people. I was pondering where shots of long stretches of deserted beaches had been found for the misleading ads when a car pulled in to Tonya's reserved parking space across the street.

"That's her," Bill said after a tall woman, dressed in denim shorts, flip-flops and a form-fitting T-shirt, climbed from the car.

He put the SUV in Drive, crossed the road and eased into a visitor's slot. We hurried from the car, followed Tonya up the stairs and approached her as she was unlocking her door.

"Ms. McClain?" Bill called before she could step inside.

Startled, the woman turned to face us.

I'd never met Tonya, so I was surprised when Bill added, "Sorry, I thought you were Tonya McClain."

The woman smiled and shrugged her shoulders. "No problem. I get that a lot. I'm Candace, her younger sister."

If this woman was younger, Tonya was definitely no spring chicken. Her sister's face, deeply tanned with wrinkles at the corners of her eyes and bracketing her mouth, wore the harried expression of someone overwhelmed and in a hurry.

Bill introduced us. "We need to speak to Tonya."

Candace shook her head. "She's not here. She's at my house."

"Her office said she called in sick," I said. "Has she been with you all day?"

"Only since mid-afternoon. I came and picked her up after she twisted her ankle. What's this all about?"

"Someone tried to kill her former boss this afternoon," Bill said.

Candace's eyes widened. "Kimberly Ross?"

Bill nodded. "We thought Tonya could help us narrow down some suspects."

She looked at me and back to Bill. "You're cops?"

"Private investigators," I said. "We're working for Ms. Ross."

Candace's expression hardened. "And you suspect Tonya because she wasn't at work today."

"The Clearwater Police have tried contacting her," Bill explained, "but she wasn't answering her door or her phone."

Candace grimaced. "She took cold medicine this

morning. It knocked her out. When she came to this afternoon, she was still groggy. She tripped over an ottoman in her condo and wrenched her ankle. That's when she called me. I came over and wrapped it—I'm a physical therapist—and took her to my house so I can keep an eye on her."

"You mind if we talk with her?" Bill said.

Candace shook her head. "But you won't have any luck. She took more cold medication right before I came over to pick up a few of her things. She'll be out like a light for another eight hours."

"Maybe we could stop by in the morning," I said. "Could we have your address?"

Candace rattled off a house number and street in a nearby subdivision. "Now, if you'll excuse me, I want to pick up Tonya's belongings and hurry home. My husband's watching the kids, and it's long past dinnertime for all of them."

Candace opened the door, stepped into the condo and closed the door behind her. Bill and I headed back to his car.

"You think she's telling the truth?" I asked.

He nodded. "As she knows it."

I thought for a moment. "Tonya could have gone to our house, accosted Trish, then twisted her ankle while making her escape."

"It's a possibility."

"Or, sometimes, as Freud supposedly said, a cigar is just a cigar."

Bill pulled me into the shadow of an overhanging bottlebrush tree. "I love it when you turn philosophical on me."

He kissed me soundly and released me only at the sound of Tonya's front door slamming above us. I was wishing Candace had taken longer on her errand when he whispered in my ear.

"Come on. We'll follow her home."

WE SPENT THE NIGHT staked out across the street from Candace's suburban bungalow. The lights went out at ten. No signs of life were visible until her husband, a short man, dressed in boxer shorts and T-shirt and built like a fire hydrant, came out the front door the next morning and walked to the end of the driveway to pick up his newspaper. Two youngsters with backpacks emerged a little after seven and joined their friends at the corner. When a county school bus arrived ten minutes later, the entire group piled on board.

Shortly afterward, Candace's garage door opened, and her husband backed out in a black SUV and drove away, presumably to work.

I stretched as well as I could, sitting down, and hoped for Adler to show up soon so Bill and I could leave and find a restroom.

As if in answer to a prayer, Adler and Ralph pulled in behind us in their unmarked car. Adler exited the passenger side, strolled to Bill's SUV and climbed into the backseat.

"You guys are probably ready for breakfast," Adler said. "We can take over from here."

I had already explained to Adler earlier by phone what Candace had told us about Tonya's activities yesterday.

"You going to question her?" I asked.

Adler nodded. "But if Tonya was the intruder, she's not going to tell us. We'll ask a few questions, then leave and watch what she does."

"Any word from Omaha on Steve Haggerty?" Bill asked.

"Yep. Their detectives claim his car isn't at his apartment."

"He could have left it at the airport," I said, "in long-term parking."

"Possible," Adler said, "but the hotels in Denali National Park have no Haggerty registered."

"Maybe he's traveling across Alaska," Bill said, "and hasn't reached the park yet."

Adler frowned. "He hasn't used his credit cards anywhere in the past few weeks."

"Could be he pays cash," I said, "or uses traveler's checks."

"One thing for sure," Adler said, "if Haggerty's wandering the back roads of Alaska, we'll have a heck of a time tracking him down. When's he due back to work?"

"A couple of weeks," I said, "according to Kim."

"So." Bill scrubbed his hand across his mouth. "Our assailant could have been McClain or Haggerty. And we don't have enough evidence to arrest or eliminate either."

"Or," I added, "our sniper-slash-intruder could have been one of Wynona Wisdom's myriad ticked-off readers. The only thing we know for sure, thanks to the break-in at our place, is that someone really is after Kim."

"We need a snare," Adler said.

"And a decoy," I agreed. "I can pose as Kim to bait the trap."

"No!" Adler and Bill snapped in unison, so fast and loud I jumped in surprise.

Bill held up his hands in protest. "No way. Not this time, Margaret. This unknown person is a sniper. There's no way we can protect you from a killing shot at a distance."

"Bill's right," Adler said. "We can't risk your getting hurt—or worse."

The protective attitude of the two men dearest to my heart threatened to make me teary-eyed. I covered my emotions with gruffness. "Then how do we attract our killer? We can't put an ad in the newspaper."

Bill's face lit with a grin that held a shimmer of malice. "We let our prime suspects know where Kim is."

Adler looked puzzled. "If you can't protect Maggie, how do you expect to keep Kim alive?"

I knew Bill well enough to see where he was headed. "By not giving Kim's true location."

"Where will we say that she is?" Adler asked.

"That," I said with a glance at Bill, "will take some figuring."

Bill nodded in agreement.

Adler glanced across the street to Tonya's sister's house. "Ralph and I will hang around to try to interview Tonya later. Can you meet with us tomorrow morning to plan a setup?"

"Tomorrow's Saturday." Bill glanced at me. "You have any objections to postponing our cruise?"

My heart sank with disappointment, but I knew we couldn't leave in the middle of a case. "My only objection is that it gives us no excuse for not having lunch with Mother Sunday at the club."

Bill was such a sweetheart, he didn't even flinch at the prospect.

"How about meeting at nine o'clock tomorrow morning?" he asked Adler. "On my boat?"

"Works for me." Adler climbed out of Bill's car and joined Ralph.

Bill and I drove away, and in the rearview mirror, I could see Adler in the front seat of the unmarked car, digging into a box of Krispy Kremes.

"I'm sorry," I said to Bill. "I should have told you about Mother's invitation sooner. She called the condo while Kim was packing. I'd forgotten all about her until just now."

He reached across the center console and squeezed my hand. "No problem. Sunday will be a good time to tell her our news."

"News?"

He flicked his gaze briefly from the road to smile at me. "That we've set a date."

"A date?"

"For our wedding."

"That's news to me, too. When were you going to fill me in?"

"We agreed there was no reason to wait once Trish

was gone," he said. "The house is fully furnished. As soon as the back door glass is repaired, it will be move-in ready. We can even have the ceremony there, if you like."

I thought for a moment, waiting for the wave of hesitation and reservations that usually assaulted me when we discussed this final step toward commitment. They didn't come. But I did experience a thrill of anticipation.

When I didn't answer right away, his smile turned to worry. "You haven't changed your mind?"

I shook my head. If anything, Trish's recent intrusion into our lives had made me more determined than ever to marry.

"Do you have a date in mind?" I asked.

"We'll have to wrap up this case first," he said. "And even though we want things simple, we'll need some time for preparations. A couple of weeks should do it. How about October? On the fourth?"

"October fourth?" I laughed out loud at the date's significance. "That's a big ten-four, Malcolm. I'll marry you then."

"Thought you would," he said with a pleased grin. "And about damned time."

CHAPTER 23

After leaving Adler and his partner in Safety Harbor, Bill and I returned to the office to check the mail and messages. Darcy was still at her mother's and wouldn't come back to work until we gave her an all clear. We didn't want our unknown assailant accosting her at work or home to demand she reveal where Kim was staying.

Abe checked in to report that all was quiet on the river front, and Melanie called to say that she had picked up Trish at the airport and taken her straight to the rehab facility. In her hasty and brief exchange, Melanie provided no details, so we didn't know whether Trish had been checked in under duress or of her own accord.

With no other cases pending, we had no reason to hang around the office, so Bill had driven me to my condo long enough to pack some clothes. The place seemed especially empty without Roger, which I considered weird, having had the pup since only last spring. The human heart is a strange and wonderful phenomenon. It had taken mine more than twenty years to commit to Bill, but that crazy little dog had me at his first woof.

Because we'd been up all night on stakeout, we returned to Bill's boat for a long nap. With Kimberly safe and Adler interviewing Tonya, we had nothing to do until the next day, so after we awoke, we took the boat down the Intracoastal Waterway to Clearwater Beach. We docked at a motel owned by a friend of Bill's and walked to the Beachcomber restaurant for a leisurely dinner.

"I've been thinking," Bill said as we waited for our drinks.

"That's usually dangerous. What's on your mind now?"

"Do you want to be married in a church?" he asked.

I'd considered the prospect of an ecclesiastical venue, so I had a ready answer. "If we choose a church, we'll have to go through premarital counseling with the minister, schedule the sanctuary and jump through all kinds of hoops. Not to mention the fact that Mother might not be able to resist taking over in such a setting. How about a justice of the peace?"

He smiled and his eyes twinkled. "Or a notary?"

"Our in-house one?" Darcy had become a notary

to facilitate documenting papers at the office. "You think she'll agree?"

"It's a big responsibility," Bill said with a serious expression. "Think how she'll feel if the marriage doesn't work out."

I felt a flutter of panic. "You think it might not?"

Bill reached across the table and took my hand. "When you marry your best friend and you've been in love for decades, how could it not work?"

Reassured, I nodded in agreement. "You want me to ask Darcy?"

"We'll ask her together, once it's safe for her to come back to the office."

AFTER DINNER, WE enjoyed a moonlight cruise on our trip back to Bill's slip at the Pelican Bay Marina and, after a delicious interval of lovemaking, snuggled into Bill's wide berth for a good night's sleep.

Bill in my arms and a comfortable bed. My life was complete. The only thing absent was Roger, who, I was sure, was having the time of his life at the river and not missing me at all.

ADLER AND PORTER showed up exactly at nine the next morning, and Bill welcomed them aboard with freshly brewed coffee and a box of Greek pastries he'd purchased at Sophia's after the nearby restaurant had opened for breakfast.

The morning breeze, although muggy, had a tang of salt and a hint of coolness, so we sat on the deck and watched the pleasure boats cruising in the channel and tourists feeding the seagulls and pelicans at the end of the nearby fishing pier.

"Any luck with your interview of Tonya McClain yesterday?" I asked.

Porter dumped cream in his coffee and shook his head. "Her story matches what she told her sister and her sister told you. She did have watery eyes and a runny nose, so the having-a-cold part of her story checks out."

"But she still could have been well enough to have broken into our house," I said.

Porter shrugged. "We have no proof, one way or the other."

"I've been thinking," Adler said between bites of baklava. "We need a place for our trap that's inaccessible to a sniper. If our killer takes a long-range shot, he'll be gone before we even figure out which direction the shot came from."

"What about here?" Bill asked.

"On the *Ten-Ninety-Eight*?" Porter asked.

Bill nodded.

I did a three-hundred-and-sixty-degree scan of the familiar site. "No tall buildings in the vicinity, dozens of boats between here and the marina park to block a clean shot and the Pram Club's building across the channel between this slip and the open water protects from a sniper in a boat on the sound."

Bill shook his head. "An accomplished sniper might figure out a way to take a shot, but I'm guessing, if we bait the trap right, our killer will try a more direct approach."

"Like he did at your house," Adler said.

I nodded. "He—or she—has already made two mistakes, first by killing Sister Mary Theresa, and second by accosting Trish. My guess is that the third time, the assailant will want to make certain he has the right woman before he strikes."

"And the only way to be certain," Porter said, "is a face-to-face confrontation."

Adler reached for another piece of baklava. "How do we accomplish up close and personal without putting either Miss Ross or a decoy at risk?"

"We give specifics to our suspects," Bill said. "Lead them to believe that Kim is staying on this boat, and that she's so certain it's safe, she's not afraid to be alone here."

"How do we do that?" Porter asked.

"We apologize to Tonya McClain," I said, "for suspecting her and let the info slip that Kim's staying here, pretending to assure Tonya that her former boss is safe."

"What about Haggerty?" Adler said. "We can't tell him if we don't know where he is."

"He checks in with Kim's office every day," I explained. "Kim can tell the office staff to fill him in on her whereabouts the next time he calls and assure him that she's all right."

"Her staff work weekends?" Adler asked.

I shook my head. "We'll have her call them first thing on Monday. That will give us time to set up here."

"Speaking of here," Adler said, glancing past the pilings at the surrounding boats and open dock, "how do we keep an eye on Bill's boat without sticking out like sore thumbs?"

"I know the owners of the boats in the slips nearest mine," Bill said. "None of them lives aboard. I'm sure we can talk them into letting us board their vessels to keep watch on mine."

"And how do we convince our killer that Kim's really aboard?" Porter asked.

"Lights on timers," Bill said, "and Maggie and I coming and going with supplies. We'll keep the curtains drawn so no one can tell what's really going on inside."

Adler grabbed a paper napkin, wiped his hands and picked up his coffee cup. "Only one problem. This isn't our jurisdiction."

"You'll have to coordinate with Deputy Do-Right," I said.

"Who?" Porter asked, and Adler choked on a mouthful of coffee.

"That's Darcy's pet name for Keating at the sheriff's department," I explained.

"I'm sure he won't give us a problem," Adler said.

I threw him an evil grin. "If Keating's involved, just don't expect to claim credit if we collar our killer."

"Maggie, Maggie," Adler said with a shake of his head. "If you taught me anything, it's that who gets the credit doesn't matter, as long as we catch the bad guys."

"You coordinate with Keating," Bill suggested to Adler, "and Maggie and I will contact the owners of the adjacent boats for permission to board and set up our surveillance."

"Sounds good." Adler stood and cast a longing look at the remaining pastries.

"Take those with you," I said.

"You sure?"

"Yeah, if you'll be dealing with Keating, you'll need your strength. And your patience."

Bill handed Adler the half-full box. "How about meeting here Monday morning to finalize our plans?"

"Seven o'clock?" Porter asked.

Bill nodded. "And I'll cook breakfast."

Adler grinned at me. "You're a lucky girl, Maggie."

"You've had your own share of luck," I told him.

"Let's just hope all this luck," Porter said, "spills over into helping us solve this case."

CHAPTER 24

Sunday lunch at the Pelican Bay Yacht Club with Mother was not as bad an ordeal as I'd anticipated. I'd worn a dress Mother had given me, so she had no reason to disapprove of my appearance. Bill looked exceptionally handsome in his well-cut blue blazer, white turtleneck and khaki slacks. For once, I didn't feel like an alien among the rich and famous of Pelican Bay.

My sister Caroline and her husband Hunt joined us and helped navigate over rough spots in the conversation. The major rocky terrain was Mother's reaction to the announcement of our wedding date.

"But that's too soon," she said with a disapproving shake of her head that didn't disturb a strand of her expertly coiffed thick white hair. "I won't have time to plan."

I started feeling queasy at the thought of Mother taking over our nuptials.

Bill, however, came straight to the rescue, bathing

Mother in the glow of his killer smile. "But that's the whole point, Priscilla. You're covered up with plans for your Queen of Hearts gala in February. All you have to do for our wedding is to show up and enjoy yourself."

"I don't know…"

Mother hated not having control over every aspect of her life and, by extension, the lives of her daughters, another result of her insecurities.

"There is one thing you could do," I said.

Her scowl disappeared and her expression brightened.

"Ask Estelle to bake our wedding cake," I said.

Mother smiled. "I know just the thing, a Lady Baltimore cake. Estelle makes such a luscious filling. But what size? And how do you want it decorated?"

"I'll leave that up to you and Estelle," I said. "You have such wonderful taste, Mother, I know whatever you choose will be stunning."

"How many guests are you expecting?" Mother asked.

"Just you, Estelle, Caroline and Hunt," I said, "and the notary who'll do the ceremony and our friends Dave and Sharon Adler and their daughter. We want a simple wedding with just family and our closest friends."

Having been given a role, no matter how small,

appeared to mollify Mother, and she was charming for the rest of the luncheon.

After the meal, Bill and I left the clubhouse. I was filled with elation at having survived the occasion with minimum friction.

"Margaret, wait!"

My luck had changed. I turned to see Caroline, hurrying across the parking lot as fast as her new pair of Prada stilettos would allow. With a sigh, I waited for her to catch up.

"I brought you something from New York," she said breathlessly.

"You did?" Her hands were empty. I glanced at the expensive bag that matched her shoes and was slung across her shoulder. If her gift was in there, it was tiny.

"I don't have it with me, silly. It's way too big to carry around."

I was afraid to ask but plunged ahead and bit the bullet. "What is it?"

"Why, your wedding dress, of course. And accessories, shoes, stockings and all. I can't let you get married in just any old thing."

Visions of plum-colored ruffles and lacy froufrou danced in my head, and I felt slightly nauseous. I should have known the luncheon had gone too well, that there had to have been a catch.

"You'll *love* it." Caroline gave me a hug. "I'll bring it by your place next week, so you'll have plenty of time for alterations.

I was considering how I might persuade Roger to alter it beyond repair when she released me. Tears glistened in her eyes.

"I can't believe it. My baby sister getting married."

Caroline fumbled in her purse for a tissue, blew her nose and returned to the club's entrance, where the valet was delivering their Town Car to a waiting Hunt.

I experienced a sudden surge of affection for my bossy older sister.

But then I hadn't seen the dress yet.

TWO DAYS LATER, I sat belowdecks on the boat in the slip across from the *Ten-Ninety-Eight* and moved closer to the porthole, trying to balance my desperate need for fresh air with the necessity of remaining out of sight. Blair Sisco, the boat's owner, had agreed to let Bill and me set up a stakeout on his Morgan sailboat in our trap for Kim's assailant.

Keeping watch on the divorced banker's boat had seemed like a good idea—until Bill had taken me below. The cabin smelled like a high school locker room with an added overlay of stale cigar smoke and the stench of stale beer. The *Risky Business* was obviously a floating party pad, one that hadn't been cleaned since the last orgy. While its exterior was shipshape, the inside resembled a frat house at the end of the semester. Bill and I had come aboard before dawn, and my stomach couldn't take much more of the oppressive atmosphere.

After briefing Kim early yesterday on what to tell her staff and making sure that Adler had informed Tonya McClain of Kim's alleged whereabouts, Bill and I had delivered groceries, mail and office supplies to the *Ten-Ninety-Eight* at odd hours, calling out greetings to an imaginary Kim as we entered. On Sunday, Bill had closed the curtains and set the lights on timers. Throughout the next day and Monday night, Adler, Porter and Keating and a couple of sheriff's deputies, all dressed as boaters, had kept watch aboard the *Risky Business* and a cabin cruiser, *Dad's Obsession*, docked in the slip alongside Bill's boat. Bill and I had relieved the sheriff's deputies on the Morgan before daylight this morning. To my relief, Keating had decided to keep watch with Adler and Porter. Having Bill around apparently took all the detective's fun out of flirting with me.

I was beginning to believe that the intruder who'd been looking for Kim was neither Tonya nor Haggerty.

So far, the person whom Trish had described, tall and gangly with loose-fitting clothes, hadn't made an appearance. I hoped whoever it was showed up soon, because with the rising sun came more heat, and the increased temperature accentuated the stench below deck. Between the malodorous surroundings and the gentle rocking of the boat as other vessels came and went in the marina, I was ready to toss my breakfast.

"Breathe through your mouth." Bill reminded me of the technique we'd used at ripening crime scenes and autopsies.

"Any Vaseline in the medicine cabinet in the head?" Stuffing my nostrils with the lubricant, another handy method from my police days, would block the stench.

"I'll check."

Bill rose from the bunk across from mine, but I grabbed his hand to stop him.

"Listen," I whispered.

I could hear the thrum of approaching footsteps on the dock.

Bill knelt on the bunk beside me, and we stared out the porthole at an oblique angle that gave us a view of the *Ten-Ninety-Eight*'s stern without divulging our presence.

The footsteps sounded louder. Their producer came

into view and stopped at the back of Bill's boat, as if reading the name emblazoned on the stern. Wearing loose slacks, deck shoes, a long-sleeve safari-style shirt, sunglasses and a ball cap pulled low over the forehead, the person could have been a man or a large woman. After a pause and a glance around as if checking to see if he—or she—were being watched, he stepped to the catwalk that ran alongside the *Ten-Ninety-Eight* and from there jumped quickly to the stern. Again he looked over his shoulder, then raised the hem of his shirt and removed a large hunting knife from a scabbard at his belt. With his other hand, he slid open the door to the lounge and disappeared inside.

Bill and I leaped from the bunk, raced topside and climbed onto the dock at the rear of Bill's boat. Adler, Porter and Keating, guns drawn, piled out of *Dad's Obsession* and joined us. Because Bill and I were along only as extra surveillance, we left the firepower to law enforcement. When our suspect exited the *Ten-Ninety-Eight*, whose slip was at the end of the dock, he'd find himself blocked by three armed cops and two determined P.I.s and nowhere else to go.

Or so I thought.

The suspect, apparently aware that he'd been duped, slammed open the slider and leaped to the dock before noticing he had company. With a flinch of surprise, he dropped his knife when he spotted us arrayed against him, blocking his escape. I expected him to surrender in the face of over-whelming odds. Instead, he pivoted, leaped from the boat to the dock and dived into the deep channel that led to the sound.

My response was automatic. I jumped in and landed on him coming up as I was going down. He grabbed me and dragged me deeper. My lungs were screaming for air, but I couldn't have breathed, even if I hadn't been underwater, because of his arm tight-ening around my neck.

I was in trouble and knew it, but my whole life didn't flash before my eyes. Only childhood memories of lifesaving lessons from the Iron Mistress in the freezing mountain lakes and recollections of my hand-to-hand training from the police academy. With a jam of a well-placed elbow, I forced the air from my attacker's lungs and caused him to loosen his grip. I kicked my way to the surface for a deep breath and found myself face-to-face with Bill.

"He's no match for two of us," I gasped, drew in another deep breath and joined Bill in a dive through the murky water. Each of us grabbed one of the suspect's arms and pulled him, kicking and struggling, to the surface. Adler and Porter were waiting with gaff hooks. Bill and I grabbed the handles they lowered toward us and dragged the man—his hat and sunglasses had been lost in the water, so we could see he was obviously male—choking and swearing, toward the dock.

Keating stepped forward to help haul the man onto the dock and cuff him. Bill and I swam to the nearest ladder, climbed out of the water and joined the others on the dock.

"Police brutality," the man snarled. "I wasn't doing anything wrong. Just a little sightseeing."

"Then why did you run?" Adler asked.

"You startled me."

"You got a name?" Porter asked.

With no authority to make an arrest, Bill and I stood to the side, wringing water from our clothes.

"I don't have to tell you anything," the man said with a smirk. "Like I said, I haven't done anything."

"Book him for trespassing," Bill suggested. "He was all over my boat. I'm pressing charges."

"That'll work for starters," Adler said.

"I'll take him in," Keating insisted.

"Be my guest." Adler looked over at me and grinned.

I knew how my former partner's mind worked. He'd let Keating hold the suspect on trespassing offenses till Adler was ready to press charges of his own. First, he had to find out the identity of our suspect.

"Hey, Steve," I called.

The man turned and looked at me.

"Haggerty, isn't it?" I guessed.

The man didn't answer.

"You don't have to tell me," I said. "Detective Keating will print you when he books you for kidnapping. We'll know your true identity soon enough."

"We don't have to wait for AFIS," Adler said, referring to the Automated Fingerprinting Identification System. "The Omaha police sent us Haggerty's photo from DMV. Aside from the wet hair, this guy matches Haggerty's photo."

Haggerty squared his dripping shoulders. "Okay, I'm Steve Haggerty. So what?"

"Aren't you supposed to be in Alaska?" I asked.

"I heard my boss was in trouble," he said. "I flew here to check on her."

I looked to Bill. "Sounds plausible."

Bill grinned and nodded. "Absolutely. Then Mr. Haggerty won't mind if the police search his car and luggage."

Haggerty stiffened, then winced when the movement caused the cuffs to pinch his wrists. "I sure as hell do mind."

"Again," Adler said. "Not a problem. We'll get a warrant, a handy little thing that removes all kinds of obstacles."

Keating led a glowering Haggerty off the dock. Adler and Porter followed.

Bill looked at me. "We'd better get into dry clothes. Your bag's still on the *Ten-Ninety-Eight*."

I nodded and stepped onto the boat's stern.

Bill didn't move. "You scared the crap out of me, Margaret, diving after that perp like a bloody Amazon."

I thought of all the miserable childhood summers spent under the obsessive tutelage of the Iron Mistress.

"Blame it on Mother," I said.

He cocked an eyebrow. "You didn't learn that kind of behavior from Priscilla."

"Not directly. It's a long story."

He grinned. "You can tell me in the shower while we wash off all this bay water."

CHAPTER 25

Two days later, I grabbed a carton of Kim's belongings from the trunk of my Volvo and followed her into her condo building and the elevator. She punched in the code for the penthouse floor.

"Must feel good to be going home," I said.

"Mixed emotions," she admitted. "I still can't get over Steve's trying to kill me. You're sure his arrest isn't a mistake?"

I felt sorry for her. She'd trusted Haggerty, counted him as a friend and named him as her successor. His treachery had cut deeply.

"There's no mistake," I said. "Detective Adler found the rifle that killed Sister Mary Theresa in the trunk of Haggerty's rental car."

"Steve's too smart to leave incriminating evidence lying around. Maybe someone put it there to frame him."

She was grasping at straws. Conspiracy theories were easier to handle than the truth.

"Steve confessed," I reminded her gently. "He kept the gun in case he needed it again, for you. But if it's any comfort, he is filled with remorse. He said he didn't have a choice. It was either kill you for the key man insurance policy to pay off the loan shark he owed or be killed himself."

The elevator doors slid open. Kim crossed the foyer, set down the luggage she was carrying and fumbled in her purse for her keys. She opened the door, dragged her bags inside, entered the living room and collapsed into the nearest chair. I followed and deposited the carton I was carrying on the coffee table.

"On the positive side," I reminded her, "you won't have to live the rest of your life looking over your shoulder."

Kim managed a weak grin. "Assuming all the wackos who pen death threats leave me alone."

I took a deep breath and let it out. "This might sound presumptuous, me giving Wynona Wisdom advice, but here's my best shot: life doesn't come with guarantees. Every cop knows that, down to the marrow in his bones. I've seen too many people who were simply in the wrong place at the wrong time and got their ticket punched early, when they should have led long, happy lives. Doesn't matter if you're

Wynona Wisdom or an average Jill with nutcase neighbors. You never know what life's going to throw at you. So you can spend what time you have, cowering with your head down, or you can treat life like the adventure it is, sucking up every drop of happiness while you have the chance."

Kim cocked her head and peered at me through her wire-framed glasses. "That's a great philosophy of yours."

I shook my head. "Not mine. It took me years to learn it."

"Where? In a book?"

I smiled. "Better. From the man I'm going to marry. And he practices what he preaches."

Kim pushed to her feet and hugged me. "Thanks, Maggie, for everything. I don't know how I can repay you."

I laughed. "By promising to counsel me if my matrimonial road gets rocky."

She walked me to the door. "Doesn't matter how rocky the road is, as long as you and Bill walk it together."

I DROVE FROM SAND KEY to Pelican Bay and the Lassiter house on Tangerine Street. Violet welcomed me at the door and led me to the back porch, where

Bessie sat, knitting what looked like a sweater. In the sweltering heat of late September, I couldn't imagine anyone needing such a heavy garment.

"It's for J.D.," Bessie explained. "Father Tom. It gets cold in New York, you know."

Violet sighed. "Such a dear man. We really miss him."

"Father Tom is the reason I'm here," I said.

"You've heard from him?" Bessie asked.

I nodded. "Indirectly. When he went missing, his children put up the money for a reward. Because you both were so kind to him, they wanted you to have it."

The white lie glided easily off my tongue. The check, made out to me, had arrived this morning from the Rochester police department. I'd taken it to the bank and had a cashier's check made out to Violet and Bessie. I handed Violet the envelope.

When she opened it and removed the check, she sank into a chair beside Bessie. For once, the loquacious older sister was speechless.

"Let me see." Bessie leaned over and took the paper from her sister's hand. "Twenty-five thousand dollars! Why, we're rich."

"We can't take it." Violet snatched the check from Bessie and thrust it toward me. "Not for merely doing our Christian duty."

I ignored the check in her outstretched hand. "Not many others would have been as kind as you were to a homeless stranger. Besides, Father Tom's children have done well for themselves. They can afford to be generous. And they're delighted to have their father back healthy and whole."

"Let's keep it, Violet." Bessie clapped her hands in excitement. "We can get our telephone back. And maybe even buy a car."

"Don't be silly," Violet snapped. "If we do keep it, we'll do something responsible with it."

Bessie narrowed her eyes at her sibling. "Like what?"

"Like putting it in the bank for our old age, that's what!"

I slipped out the screen door and headed to my car, while the sisters were still arguing over a use for their windfall. I couldn't help smiling. In spite of their feisty discussions, Violet and Bessie were devoted to each other, and the reward money from Father Tom's children had provided a sorely needed financial cushion for the elderly women.

The tears in my eyes surprised me. As a cop, I'd witnessed too many crimes against humanity and too few happy endings. But, in this case, I should have expected otherwise. Father Tom, after all, had friends in high places.

The signs for my wedding day were auspicious. I awoke without prenuptial jitters or misgivings—until I remembered that Mother would be attending the ceremony. I hadn't seen or heard from her since our luncheon at the club, but, knowing her need for control, I shuddered to think what she'd planned behind the scenes, ready to spring on me when I least expected it.

Caroline, however, had shown up at my condo the day after I'd last visited the Lassiters. I opened the door to find her juggling shopping bags and dress boxes.

"We've got work to do." She breezed down the hallway and into the living room and deposited her packages onto the sofa.

Roger, at the sound of Caroline's voice, abandoned his welcoming happy dance, hightailed it to the kitchen and hid beneath the table.

My stomach knotted as I watched the flurry of

tissue paper through which Caroline dug like a diver plunging for pearls. From the names of the shops and designers on the bags and boxes, I could tell my sister had spent a small fortune. And from past experience, I knew I was going to hate whatever she'd chosen. However, faced with the choice of having the wedding I wanted or hurting my sister's feelings, I'd choose the latter. I intended to marry only once, and I wouldn't allow family pressures, guilty conscience or insecurities to spoil the occasion.

When Caroline turned from her shopping booty and held up the dress she'd selected, my jaw dropped and I sank into the nearest chair.

"It's beautiful," I stammered through my shock.

The simple sleeveless dress in silk the pale coral of a Florida sunset was stunning, something I'd have chosen myself, if I could have afforded it.

Caroline flashed a self-satisfied smirk. "I thought you'd like it. It's very *you*, Margaret, no-nonsense but obvious quality. And that's not all."

From the deep dress box, she pulled a matching coat with a mandarin collar.

I loved it, but I was still without words.

"Now," she said, "the shoes."

I winced, picturing another pair of torturous stilet- tos like the last pair she'd had me buy. Those must have been designed by a desperate podiatrist hoping to drum up business. To my relief, she pulled out a pair of pumps in Italian leather the same pale coral as the dress—with two-inch heels.

"I had them dyed to match," Caroline said.

"They're perfect." My eyes were tearing up again. My stylish sister wouldn't be caught dead in such shoes, but she'd bought me exactly what I'd wanted.

"Try them on," she said. "No, wait. I forgot the veil."

"Veil?" Her selections had been too perfect. I should have known there would be a catch. "I can't wear a veil, not with this outfit."

She reached for a hatbox. "It's not really a veil. Remember the sixties? We used to call them whimsies. I had a milliner whip this up." After digging through more tissue paper, she extracted a tiny wisp of tulle in pale coral, shaped to fit loosely over my hair like a large cloche and accented with several tiny silk bows that matched the dress. "What do you think?"

I sprang from the chair and hugged Caroline, who barely managed to save the whimsy from my crushing embrace. "Everything is too beautiful. How can I thank you?"

I'd sold my sister short and was suffering pangs of guilt for my lowered expectations.

Caroline returned my hug, then released me. "Just be happy, Margaret. You deserve it." She cleared her throat of the huskiness that had colored her words. "Now, go try it all on. Let's see if everything fits."

WE GATHERED AT OUR house the evening of the ceremony, and I appreciated Caroline's gift even more when I saw the expression on Bill's face when he first glimpsed me. My knees went weak at the love in his eyes, and I feared for an instant I might have to be married sitting down.

The other guests had already arrived when Hunt, Caroline and I pulled up in the Town Car. Our house was gleaming and awash with light. Bill had strung strands of white twinkle lights in the weeping elm on the patio where the ceremony would take place. Delicious aromas emanated from the kitchen, informing me that Estelle, bless her, had done much more than bake the fabulous three-tiered cake that centered the dining table. It was topped with a miniature nosegay of ivory-colored roses, the same hue as the bouquet Bill handed me.

My husband-to-be was not only thoughtful, but a diplomat, too. He'd provided corsages for all the women, making certain Mother's was the biggest and most elaborate. Even little Jessica had a tiny wrist corsage. Hunt and Adler wore boutonnieres that matched the one in the lapel of Bill's navy blue suit.

Roger, who loved people almost as much as food, wandered from guest to guest, sniffing shoes and ankles and submitting to pats and praises. I tensed when I saw him approach Mother, who didn't like dogs, but Estelle saved the day. For the rest of the evening, whenever Roger neared Mother, Estelle snagged a cheese straw from the plate on the dining table and diverted Roger's attention with the tasty treat. Soon, he refused to move farther than arm's length from Estelle, his new best friend.

The only unpleasant surprise was the photographer Mother had hired to document the proceedings. Bill thanked Mother for her thoughtfulness, then drew the photographer aside and apparently threatened him with bodily harm if his picture-taking became the least intrusive, because the poor guy, in spite of glaring looks from Mother, remained discreetly in the background.

The sun was setting, turning the western sky the same shade as my wedding dress, when we gathered on the patio for the brief ceremony. Darcy was more nervous than either the bride or groom. With two decades of love, friendship and knowledge of each other's qualities and foibles, Bill and I had faith in the strength of our relationship. I'd debated long and hard over this decision and, as Bill slipped the plain yellow gold band on my finger, I reveled in the rightness of it.

Adler was first to claim the right to kiss the bride. "Be happy, Maggie," he whispered in my ear. "You're a special lady, and Bill's a lucky guy."

I hugged my former partner. "I'm the lucky one."

HOURS LATER, WHEN the guests had left, Bill and I sat together on the sofa in the living room and finished the last of the champagne. Bill had stripped off his jacket and loosened his tie. I'd shed whimsy, duster and shoes and propped my stockinged feet on the coffee table. Roger curled next to me, sleepy and sated with cheese straws.

"I thought the evening went well," Bill said.

I nodded. "In spite of the unexpected photographer."

"We'll be glad later to have the pictorial record."

"Mother even behaved herself," I said. "No disparaging remarks about our house or our ceremony."

"It got a little dicey when she started planning the fancy reception at the club," Bill said.

I smiled at my new husband. "But you handled her brilliantly. I didn't know we were planning an imminent around-the-world cruise that will take months. I thought we were going to the Caribbean for a few weeks on the *Ten-Ninety-Eight*."

"Did I forget to tell you?" His blue eyes sparkled with mischief.

"And I thought I was marrying an honest man."

"We'll start out around the world, but we'll come home when we're ready, even if we go only as far as the Caribbean. If my fib gives us a chance to enjoy our newly married status without Priscilla's machinations, so much the better."

I leaned into the circle of his embrace, happy and content. "I'm ready for bed."

"Tired?" he asked.

I shook my head. "Not a bit. In fact, I don't think I'll sleep a wink tonight."

Bill set aside his champagne flute, stood, scooped me into his arms and carried me to the bedroom. Our bedroom.

"Good thing, then," he said with a grin filled with love and promise, "that I'm here to keep you company."

I snuggled against his shoulder and tightened my arms around his neck. "We're in this together now, for the long haul."

"Hallelujah," Bill said with a laugh, and kicked the bedroom door shut behind us.

* * * * *

**Every Life Has More
Than One Chapter**

Award-winning author Stevi Mittman delivers
another hysterical mystery, featuring Teddi Bayer,
an irrepressible heroine, and her to-die-for hero,
Detective Drew Scoones. After all, life on Long
Island can be murder!

*Turn the page for a sneak peek
at the warm and funny fourth book,*
WHOSE NUMBER IS UP, ANYWAY?,
in the Teddi Bayer series,
by STEVI MITTMAN.
On sale August 7

"Before redecorating a room, I always advise my clients to empty it of everything but one chair. Then I suggest they move that chair from place to place, sitting in it, until the placement feels right. Trust your instincts when deciding on furniture placement. Your room should 'feel right.'"
—TipsFromTeddi.com

Gut feelings. You know, that gnawing in the pit of your stomach that warns you that you are about to do the absolute stupidest thing you could do? Something that will ruin life as you know it?

I've got one now, standing at the butcher counter in King Kullen, the grocery store in the same strip mall as L.I. Lanes, the bowling alley-cum-billiard parlor I'm in the process of redecorating for its "Grand Opening."

I realize being in the wrong supermarket probably doesn't sound exactly dire to you, but you aren't the one buying your father a brisket at a store your mother will somehow know isn't Waldbaum's.

And then, June Bayer isn't your mother.

The woman behind the counter has agreed to go into the freezer to find a brisket for me, since there aren't any in the case. There are packages of pork tenderloin, piles of spare ribs and rolls of sausage, but no briskets.

Warning Number Two, right? I should be so out of here.

But no, I'm still in the same spot when she comes back out, brisketless, her face ashen. She opens her mouth as if she is going to scream, but only a gurgle comes out.

And then she pinballs out from behind the counter, knocking bottles of Peter Luger Steak Sauce to the floor on her way, now hitting the tower of cans at the end of the prepared foods aisle and sending them sprawling, now making her way down the aisle, careening from side to side as she goes.

Finally, from a distance, I hear her shout, "He's deeeeeeaaaad! Joey's deeeeeaaaad."

My first thought is, *You should always trust your gut.*

My second thought is that now, somehow, my mother will know I was in King Kullen. For weeks I will have to hear "What did you expect?" as though whenever you go to King Kullen someone turns up dead. And if the detective investigating the case turns out to be Detective Drew Scoones…well, I'll never hear the end of that from her, either.

She still suspects I murdered the guy who was found dead on my doorstep last Halloween just to get Drew back into my life.

Several people head for the butcher's freezer and I position myself to block them. If there's one thing I've learned from finding people dead—and the guy on my doorstep wasn't the first one—it's that the police get very testy when you mess with their murder scenes.

"You can't go in there until the police get here," I say, stationing myself at the end of the butcher's counter and in front of the Employees Only door, acting as if I'm some sort of authority. "You'll contaminate the evidence if it turns out to be murder."

Shouts and chaos. You'd think I'd know better than to throw the word *murder* around. Cell phones are flipping open and tongues are wagging.

I amend my statement quickly. "Which, of course, it probably isn't. Murder, I mean. People die all the time, and it's not always in hospitals or their own beds, or…" I babble when I'm nervous, and the idea of someone dead on the other side of the freezer door makes me very nervous.

So does the idea of seeing Drew Scoones again.

Drew and I have this on-again, off-again sort of thing…that I kind of turned off.

Who knew he'd take it so personally when he tried to get serious and I responded by saying we could talk about *us* tomorrow—and then caught a plane to my parents' condo in Boca the next day? In July. In the middle of a job.

For some crazy reason, he took that to mean that I was avoiding him and the subject of *us*.

That was three months ago. I haven't seen him since.

The manager, who identifies himself and points to his nameplate in case I don't believe him, says he has to go into *his cooler*. "Maybe Joey's not dead," he says. "Maybe he can be saved, and you're letting him die in there. Did you ever think of that?"

In fact, I hadn't. But I had thought that the murderer might try to go back in to make sure his tracks were covered, so I say that I will go in and check.

Which means that the manager and I couple up and go in together while everyone pushes against the doorway to peer in, erasing any chance of finding clean prints on that Employees Only door.

I expect to find carcasses of dead animals hanging from hooks, and maybe Joey hanging from one, too.

I think it's going to be very creepy and I steel myself, only to find a rather benign series of shelves with large slabs of meat laid out carefully on them, along with boxes and boxes marked simply Chicken.

Nothing scary here, unless you count the body of a middle-aged man with graying hair sprawled faceup on the floor. His eyes are wide open and unblinking. His shirt is stiff. His pants are stiff. His body is stiff. And his expression, you should forgive the pun—is frozen. Bill-the-manager crosses himself and stands mute while I pronounce the guy dead in a sort of *happy now?* tone.

"We should not be in here," I say, and he nods his head emphatically and helps me push people out of the doorway just in time to hear the police sirens and see the cop cars pull up outside the big store windows.

Bobbie Lyons, my partner in Teddi Bayer Interior Designs (and also my neighbor, my best friend and my private fashion police), and Mark, our carpenter (and my dogsitter, confidant and ego booster), rush in from next door. They beat the cops by a half step and shout out my name. People point in my direction.

After all the publicity that followed the unfortunate incident during which I shot my ex-husband, Rio Gallo, and then the subsequent murder of my first client—which I solved, I might add—it seems like the whole world, or at least all of Long Island, knows who I am.

Mark asks if I'm all right. (Did I remember to mention that the man is drop-dead-gorgeous-but-a-decade-too-young-for-me-yet-too-old-for-my-daughter-thank-god?) I don't get a chance to answer him because the police are quickly closing in on the store manager and me.

"The woman—" I begin telling the police. Then I have to pause for the manager to fill in her name, which he does: *Fran*.

I continue. "Right. Fran. Fran went into the freezer to get a brisket. A moment later she came out and screamed that Joey was dead. So I'd say she was the one who discovered the body."

"And you are…?" the cop asks me. It comes out a bit like who do I *think* I am, rather than who am I really?

"An innocent bystander," Bobbie, hair perfect, makeup just right, says, carefully placing her body between the cop and me.

"And she was just leaving," Mark adds. They each take one of my arms.

Fran comes into the inner circle surrounding the cops. In case it isn't obvious from the hairnet and bloodstained white apron with Fran embroidered on it, I explain that she was the butcher who was going for the brisket. Mark and Bobbie take that as a signal that I've done my job and they can now get me out of there. They twist around, with me in the middle, as if we're a Rockettes line, until we are facing away from the butcher counter. They've managed to propel me a few steps toward the exit when disaster—in the form of a Mazda RX7 pulling up at the loading curb—strikes.

Mark's grip on my arm tightens like a vise. "Too late," he says.

Bobbie's expletive is unprintable. "Maybe there's a back door," she suggests, but Mark is right. It's too late.

I've laid my eyes on Detective Scoones. And while my gut is trying to warn me that my heart shouldn't go there, regions farther south are melting at just the sight of him.

"Walk," Bobbie orders me.

And I try to. Really.

Walk, I tell my feet. *Just put one foot in front of the other*.

I can do this because I know, in my heart of hearts, that if Drew Scoones was still interested in me, he'd have gotten in touch with me after I returned from Boca. And he didn't.

Since he's a detective, Drew doesn't have to wear

one of those dark blue Nassau County Police uniforms. Instead, he's got on jeans, a tight-fitting T-shirt and a tweedy sports jacket. If you think that sounds good, you should see him. Chiseled features, cleft chin, brown hair that's naturally a little sandy in the front, a smile that...well, that doesn't matter. He isn't smiling now.

He walks up to me, tucks his sunglasses into his breast pocket and looks me over from head to toe.

"Well, if it isn't Miss Cut and Run," he says. "Aren't you supposed to be somewhere in Florida or something?" He looks at Mark accusingly, as if he was covering for me when he told Drew I was gone.

"Detective Scoones?" one of the uniforms says. "The stiff's in the cooler and the woman who found him is over there." He jerks his head in Fran's direction.

Drew continues to stare at me.

You know how when you were young, your mother always told you to wear clean underwear in case you were in an accident? And how, a little farther on, she told you not to go out in hair rollers because you never knew who you might see—or who might see you? And how now your best friend says she wouldn't be caught dead without makeup and suggests you shouldn't, either?

Okay, today, *finally,* in my overalls and Converse sneakers, I get it.

I brush my hair out of my eyes. "Well, I'm back," I say. As if he hasn't known my exact whereabouts. The man is a detective, for heaven's sake. "Been back awhile."

Bobbie has watched the exchange and apparently decided she's given Drew all the time he deserves. "And we've got work to do, so…" she says, grabbing my arm and giving Drew a little two-fingered wave goodbye.

As I back up a foot or two, the store manager sees his chance and places himself in front of Drew, trying to get his attention. Maybe what makes Drew such a good detective is his ability to focus.

Only what he's focusing on is me.

"Phone broken? Carrier pigeon died?" he asks me, taking in Fran, the manager, the meat counter and that Employees Only door, all without taking his eyes off me.

Mark tries to break the spell. "We've got work to do there, you've got work to do here, Scoones," Mark says to him, gesturing toward next door. "So it's back to the alley for us."

Drew's lip twitches. "You working the alley now?" he says.

"If you'd like to follow me," Bill-the-manager, clearly exasperated, says to Drew—who doesn't respond. It's as if waiting for my answer is all he has to do.

So, fine. "You knew I was back," I say.

The man has known my whereabouts every hour of the day for as long as I've known him. And my mother's not the only one who won't buy that he "just happened" to answer this particular call. In fact, I'm willing to bet my children's lunch money that he's taken every call within ten miles of my home since the day I got back.

And now he's gotten lucky.

"*You* could have called *me*," I say.

"You're the one who said *tomorrow* for our talk and then flew the coop, chickie," he says. "I figured the ball was in your court."

"Detective?" the uniform says. "There's something you ought to see in here."

Drew gives me a look that amounts to *in or out?*

He could be talking about the investigation, or about our relationship.

Bobbie tries to steer me away. Mark's fists are balled. Drew waits me out, knowing I won't be able to resist what might be a murder investigation.

Finally he turns and heads for the cooler.

And, like a puppy dog, I follow.

Bobbie grabs the back of my shirt and pulls me to a halt.

"I'm just going to show him something," I say, yanking away.

"Yeah," Bobbie says, pointedly looking at the buttons on my blouse. The two at breast level have popped. "That's what I'm afraid of."

REQUEST YOUR FREE BOOKS!

2 FREE NOVELS PLUS 2 FREE GIFTS!

There's the life you planned. And there's what comes next.

YES! Please send me 2 FREE Harlequin® NEXT™ novels and my 2 FREE mystery gifts. After receiving them, if I don't wish to receive any more books, I can return the shipping statement marked "cancel." If I don't cancel, I will receive 4 brand-new novels every other month and be billed just $3.99 per book in the U.S. or $4.74 per book in Canada, plus 25¢ shipping and handling per book plus applicable taxes, if any.* That's a savings of over 25% off the cover price! I understand that accepting the 2 free books and gifts places me under no obligation to buy anything. I can always return a shipment and cancel at any time. Even if I never buy anything from Harlequin, the two free books and gifts are mine to keep forever.   155 HDN EL33 355 HDN EL4F

Name _____ (PLEASE PRINT) _____

Address _____ Apt. # _____

City _____ State/Prov. _____ Zip/Postal Code _____

Signature (if under 18, a parent or guardian must sign)

Order online at www.TryNEXTNovels.com

Or mail to the **Harlequin Reader Service®**:
IN U.S.A.: P.O. Box 1867, Buffalo, NY 14240-1867
IN CANADA: P.O. Box 609, Fort Erie, Ontario L2A 5X3

Not valid to current Harlequin NEXT subscribers.

Want to try two free books from another line?
Call 1-800-873-8635 or visit www.morefreebooks.com

* Terms and prices subject to change without notice. NY residents add applicable sales tax. Canadian residents will be charged applicable provincial taxes and GST. This offer is limited to one order per household. All orders subject to approval. Credit or debit balances in a customer's account(s) may be offset by any other outstanding balance owed by or to the customer. Please allow 4 to 6 weeks for delivery.

Your Privacy: Harlequin Books is committed to protecting your privacy. Our Privacy Policy is available online at www.eHarlequin.com or upon request from the Harlequin Reader Service. From time to time we make our lists of customers available to reputable firms who may have a product or service of interest to you. If you would prefer we not share your name and address, please check here. ☐

NEXT07R

REASONS FOR REVENGE

A brand-new provocative miniseries by *USA TODAY*
bestselling author **Maureen Child** begins with

SCORNED
BY THE BOSS

Jefferson Lyon is a man used to having his own way.
He runs his shipping empire from California, and
his admin Caitlyn Monroe runs the rest of his world.
When Caitlin decides she's had enough and needs
new scenery, Jefferson devises a plan to get her back.
Jefferson *never* loses, but little does he know that
he's in a competition....

Don't miss any of the other titles from the
REASONS FOR REVENGE trilogy by
USA TODAY bestselling author **Maureen Child.**

SCORNED BY THE BOSS #1816
Available August 2007

SEDUCED BY THE RICH MAN #1820
Available September 2007

CAPTURED BY THE BILLIONAIRE #1826
Available October 2007

Only from Silhouette Desire!

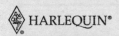

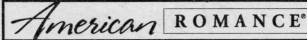

TEXAS LEGACIES: THE CARRIGANS

Get to the Heart of a Texas Family

WITH

THE RANCHER NEXT DOOR
by

Cathy Gillen Thacker

She'll Run The Ranch—And Her Life—Her Way!

On her alpaca ranch in Texas, Rebecca encounters
constant interference from Trevor McCabe, the
bossy rancher next door. Rebecca becomes very
friendly with Vince Owen, her other neighbor and
Trevor's archrival from college. Trevor's problem
is convincing Rebecca that he is on her side, and
aware of Vince's ulterior motives. But Trevor has
fallen for her in the process....

On sale July 2007

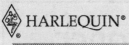

COMING NEXT MONTH

#89 WHOSE NUMBER IS UP, ANYWAY? •
Stevi Mittman

While redoing the local bowling alley, decorator
Teddi Bayer finds murder on the scorecard—members of the
bowling league are being knocked off like pins in a strike
after all chipping in to buy a winning lottery ticket. Soon
the killer targets Teddi—and detective Drew Scoones seems
too distracted by Teddi's charms to come to her rescue!

#90 DIRTY HARRIET RIDES AGAIN •
Miriam Auerbach

Harley-riding P.I. Harriet Horowitz thinks she's seen it all—
until an unusual exchange of vows gets even stranger when
the reverend turns up as a corpse before the first
"I do." There's a twisted killer on the loose in Boca, and
it's up to Harriet—with the help of stud muffin sports
trainer Lior Ben Yehuda and her pet alligator, Lana—to
crack the case.